I0635883

**The Queen's Keys**

**© 2022 F. Bradley Reaume**

Author—F. Bradley Reaume

Published by Penshurst Publishing (Books) 2022

First Edition—February 2022

This is a work of fiction set at a particular time and place in history. Situations which include known historical figures are imagined and entirely fictitious.

**ISBN # 978-1-7770810-5-8**

# The Queen's Keys

## By F. Bradley Reaume

# Chapter One - Washington DC - July 1965

The usual buzz at the center of London had stopped, replaced by the hum of anticipation. The only movement was the ponderous parade of a funeral cortege with its accompanying military escort.

Crowds lined the streets in heavy coats, hopping foot to foot in the January cold. Sporadic streaks of breath were visible by the stark winter light. Lines of spectators thickened as the procession arrived at St. Paul's Cathedral, nestled into a high spot in the oldest part of the city.

An architectural confection, Wren's masterpiece replaced an older building that had been lost in the Great Fire almost 300 years before. On this day several men gathered to meet the hearse and carry the casket up the steps and into the great building. More distinguished men of the realm were present, hovering nearby but their advanced ages required they engage a stand-in to do the actual lifting and carrying.

And then, the service complete, it was time to leave.

Queen Elizabeth stood just outside the main doors, apparently oblivious to the bitter mid-winter cold. In front of her, the coffin of Sir Winston Churchill, draped with a British Union Jack, had been carried down the steps of the great cathedral. Behind the Queen were the mighty men of England, foreign heads of state, representatives from around the world and members of her family and Churchill's.

The casket was carried by a group of British notables, who transferred it to an open gun carriage for the slow march to the Thames. There it would begin a final trip down the river, past the panoply of London, its historic buildings, famous bridges, notable vistas, its grime and working buildings, with thousands upon thousands of Londoners lining the river banks and crossings. It passed a row of large construction cranes on the river's edge, which bowed in turn as the boat and its cargo passed.

Sitting in front of a large screen, two men were watching these collected newsreels of the scene, or rather a compendium of motion picture snippets taken from the funeral. They sat in a small room equipped with the screen set furthest from the door. The screen had been unrolled, pulled down from its resting place. There was a long table and necessary chairs. The projector sat behind a framed opening high on the opposite wall. There the projectionist worked in a small room, loading and spooling requested film. Flanking the door to the hall there was a framed photo of President Linden B. Johnson and another of the United States Capital Building.

With no windows, a locked door, and an armed guard outside in the hall, the arrangement was standard operating procedure, even for this heavily guarded official building in the center of Washington, D.C. The very definition of non-descript, this six storey grey stone building was not far from the US Department of the Treasury, a mile or so from Foggy Bottom, a Washington D.C. neighbourhood built on a former swamp around a tidal pool, next

6

to the Potomac River.

"Churchill will pass through the capital along the river before being transported privately to Bladon, near Blenheim Palace, for his final internment," intoned the voice-over narrator, to pictures of the flag-draped coffin on the back of a small river launch, moving down river, into the distance. The film faded to black.

"Okay, he was born there wasn't he? Churchill's funeral, a few weeks ago, very sad. Tell me what I'm looking for, or at."

"Yes, yes, but that's not what is interesting," he said over his shoulder. "Let's see it again." He made a signal to the projectionist. "Look at these stills while they rewind the film," he slid a file folder across the table. "The photos are captured from the motion picture footage and some were taken by one of our men on the ground."

"We have men on the ground at funerals?'

"Anywhere they are deemed necessary."

The second man, in full dress uniform, dutifully reached out and opened the folder. As he shuffled through the photos his brow creased, suggesting a flicker of interest, or at least a bit of consternation at not recognizing too many of the subjects.

"Okay Anderson, enough mystery. What am I looking at?"

"That's what we wanted to know."

"Stop being so god damn obtuse."

The film began to play again, at the point the casket was being lifted up the steps of St. Paul's. The uniformed man shuffled through the stills.

"Some of these men are well known, no surprise to anyone that they were present. But not all. I spied something, so I put a few agents on it and it turns out this man," he pointed to a dark suited man standing behind the Queen, "this man spent almost the entire funeral with the Queen, subtly in the background but within speaking distance. Most irregular."

"So was her attendance at the ceremony. I understand the Queen does not attend the funerals of commoners. In fact her attendance at any funeral is quite rare, and irregular."

"Don't forget the singing of 'The Battle Hymn of the Republic' which Churchill loved. He was more than half an American it seems. Singing about the Republic, in the presence of the Queen, at a state funeral? The broken protocols lay shattered, and their shards were kicked around with glee."

"So who is the guy?"

"That's the real issue. He's apparently one of ours. He is an American by birth, German by heritage and a naturalized English subject. Here's the interesting part, we used him during the war as an observer in London, but we thought he was dead, captured or killed during an intelligence assignment into occupied France in 1941, not long after the Nazis invaded France."

The second man tilted his head downward and his eyes narrowed.

"You said he was an observer. He was an agent?"

"Not really, he was an observer for us, and it appears he was more than that to the British. We did know about his British ties and apparently they knew of his American ones. It's in the file. He was sort of an unacknowledged parallel observer. I know this, as I was his contact in London at the time."

"And he was given up for dead by us, but is apparently quite healthy and friendly with the Queen."

"He is Professor Christoph Schroeder, recruited from Penn State in the early 30's due to his German background. Lot of Germans in Pennsylvania, you know. We set him up to spend time in Germany as an academic, but as tensions rose the Nazi's kicked out anyone who had not been in the country prior to 1933. He was not terribly well suited to intelligence work, too nervous. We didn't want to just cut him loose so he was supposed to feed us with any intelligence information he found in his daily travels. We weren't expecting much. He ended up in London and we still used him to corroborate intel here and there, troop movements, construction projects, anything he heard at the University. According to the file, that stream dried up in the spring of 1941 after he went missing in France, not long after the Nazis defeated the French and were solidifying their hold on the country."

"But there he stands with the Queen, almost 25 years later."

"Ah but there is more. We were trying to extract him from France after his mission and he went missing. At the time he was being approached by the Germans and Russians as a contact in Britain. We thought it best to bring him in. Now I find he has been working under an alias at Oxford for 20 years."

The second man shrugged, his epaulets moving up in unison with his eyebrows.

"And he is now known as Professor Andrew Merrimack, and has just been named on this year's Queen's List as the new Earl of Osborne. Osborne House was the preferred home of Queen Victoria, located on the Isle of Wight, just off the southern coast near the naval base at Portsmouth." The uniformed man's eyebrows flickered up with each revelation.

"Tell me more."

"There is no more to tell. Do you want us to confront Mr. Schroeder?"

"Let me think on it. See if you can find out any more of this man's movements during the war and after. I would like an extensive dossier. Mr. Schroeder seems to be more than we thought. If the Brits brought him in, perhaps we have nothing to worry about.

Depending upon what you find I may have to inform the President."

The other man nodded as he collected up the photos, "I already have a few agents checking the records. With your approval I would like to contact the British and send a few forensic document experts to England to peruse their files. We don't want to let on we know about Schroeder, but it appears our allies have been hiding something. So we will invent some pretext. It's not an unusual thing to do."

"The pretext or the document search?"

"Both, I guess."

They shook hands. "I expect something in a week, or at least a report on why I don't have anything."

The uniformed man rose to leave, his medals clicking together. He seemed about to say something but changed his mind, "Very good, thank you."

# Chapter Two - November 1938

"Ah Professor Schroeder, so glad you could indulge me."

Winston Spenser Churchill, 64, the son of the younger brother of the Duke of Marlborough, a consummate politician and a man connected like no one in British society, sat heavily on a wooden box, the box stamped with a familiar brand of Scotch whiskey. He appeared to be a man with time on his hands, and as a back-bencher in the Conservative government of Prime Minister Neville Chamberlain, in November 1938, he had little to do with setting public policy. However he still wielded considerable influence.

His supporters pointed to his prescient successes while his detractors remembered his mistakes, even if those failures were due to factors that were beyond his control. He accepted the responsibility and left it to history to determine his culpability.

On this day he was balanced on a box which sat on the edge of a fishpond at the bottom of a small rise, which, several dozen yards away, resulted in Chartwell, his gentleman's pile of masonry in

Kent, just far enough south of London to be inconvenient.

"I am fascinated by the fish, though I don't exactly know why. Perhaps it is that they swim near the top of their 'atmosphere' while we wander about at the bottom of ours. I wonder if they comprehend the void above them in much the same way we do ours?"

Schroeder looked at Sir Winston expectantly. He had received the invitation, almost a summons to Chartwell some days before. He was going to beg off but thinking on it, and getting a word of encouragement from his department head, he changed his mind. He was not empty handed and had a small tote containing a sheaf of papers that he'd brought with him, papers relating to his area of study. He had considered leaving the papers in the car, which he had borrowed from a senior Dean at the University, the same person who had encouraged him to attend the meeting. He grabbed them as a second thought, if only to add weight to his visit.

"We are both half American, you and I. A bloody shame our parliament wasn't a mite more accommodating to the colonists when it mattered. They might still be with us."

"Oh, I think they are sir, but I will concede they only are, when their interests align with British interests."

"I note sir, that you did not say 'our interests, but rather referred to 'British interests'."

"As I am not British save perhaps by sensibility."

"But you are living in Britain. Are you German?"

"By heritage sir yes, my grandfather left Germany and arrived in America just after their Civil War. And I am proud of that heritage, however, no, I do not subscribe to the ideals of Nationalists, Socialists or Fascists. I am involved with my work at the University

12

and do not have time for politics, nor much of an inclination."

"An academic without an interest in politics? You are a rarity Professor."

"My family left Germany several generations ago because they felt much the same. The oppressive social class structure mixed with the aggressive nationalism of the Prussians was too much for my grandfather."

"But America did not suffice? So you came to England."

Schroeder laughed. "Actually I went to work in Germany, as my area of study, which is social constructs, the nobility and the stratification of society, were fairly alien concepts in America. As a speaker of German I thought I could settle easily in that country. However, the provincialism of my accent and the growing clamour for apparently, authentic Germans, forced me to England several years ago."

"There was no place for you in America, the land of opportunity?"

"Initially yes, just prior to the Depression there were possibilities in Omaha or Texas. The first one I couldn't find on a map, the second was too hot when I visited."

"Southern summers can be difficult."

"It was December."

"And so you are in England at the University of West London?"

"It seemed the best choice. I am currently the Schnellinghurst Professor of European History, a seat endowed a few generations ago by a German industrialist who married into a British academic family."

Churchill pursed his lips and gazed into the placid waters of the pond. The sound of a fish breaching the surface broke the momentary silence. Schroeder did not see the breach but looked at the pond seeking its evidence. He was surprised he could not see any ripples in the water given that the sound seemed so close.

"So, down to brass tacks Schroeder. I am in great need of help. And I must say you have come to me highly recommended for this task."

"By whom?"

" 'Whom' does not matter. 'Why?' however, might. I understand you have been tasked by the State Department in Washington to report to them on interesting facts surrounding your trips to the continent, and presumably here in England."

Schroeder blinked and his throat was instantly dry. He was caught off guard by the revelation. He swallowed hard, buying time.

"Absolutely. Washington has tasked many people overseas to be their eyes and ears. It was the same when I was in Germany."

"So presumably the Germans were correct in their determination to force you out?"

"You could draw that conclusion."

"I need you to be doing the same for England. I understand you sometimes travel to the Continent for research purposes?"

"Given the troubles brewing on the continent I am unlikely to be travelling there in the near future. Regarding my activities, I don't do anything out of the ordinary. I simply tell an American friend of mine what I see and he, I presume, passes it on. More like a trave-logue. This hotel was nice, that restaurant too crowded. I would be happy to provide you with the same reports."

"And that train carried troop vehicles, and this road was blocked off. No sir, you misunderstand me. I need you to provide reports to us, separate from those you send to Washington."

But they would be the same thing, save the British parts which I gather you would already be familiar with. And frankly, I remind you, I am unlikely to travel to the Continent in the near future."

"I'll be blunt Schroeder. I need you to travel to Europe, engage in some research in your field of study, and come back to England without mentioning the true nature of the mission to your American contacts."

"So you want me to be a double agent?"

"You just said you weren't even a single agent."  Churchill threw his head back and laughed heartily, "No, we are allies with the Americans. Think of what you might do for us to be in parallel with them, as we are striving for the same goal. I don't want them to know because, in truth, what I am asking from you is information related to a long shot, an exercise that may not pay any dividends. And if our American allies knew what we were trying, we would appear desperately weak and perhaps foolish. If we get anything substantive, I assure you it will be shared with our allies. We cannot afford to jeopardize that relationship, even if it doesn't officially exist yet. Britain is very weak, Chamberlain refuses to take the necessary preparations, and Herr Hitler and his Nazis are pushing ever harder. Their occupation of Austria is just the beginning."

"And what if my American friend calls me out? I don't want to lie and certainly do not want to invite trouble."

"Try to avoid providing details. I agree, you do not want trouble, nor do I want trouble for you. I just don't want to look desperate to our American cousins, despite the Nazi push. Tell them you are going. The trip is being set up as a research opportunity for you in your work at the University. Report to them what you see. Just do not divulge our part of your travels."

"So far the Nazis have pushed against rotten foundations, apparently, as the Austrians joined them willingly."

"I can say, as someone briefed on the matter through our intelligence channels, that it was less willing than it appeared. They might be Germanic in nature but the Austrians are more distant cousins than blood brothers. They believe the Prussians to be coarse and uncouth, and the Nazis are seen the same way by the Prussians. The aggressive tactics of the Nazis reinforce that belief."

"So you are convinced there will be war and that the Americans will enter on the Anglo-French side?"

"Oh yes, the Americans simply want to preserve the status quo, and Hitler is disturbing it profoundly. They will join us, just as they did in 1917. Better late than never."

"And we here in Britain will oppose the Germans?"

"It is long standing British policy to stand against any one country that is attempting to dominate  Europe. My own ancestor, the First Duke of Marlborough, was lauded for maintaining that balance, when we sided with the Austrians against the French."

"And what if England should become that, the unbalancer of Europe?"

"That would not happen. We are too happy here on our little island. And our detachment means our influence is limited."

"The Scots and the Welsh might disagree."

And Churchill snickered, shaking his head. "A worthy rejoinder, but even the Scots and the Welsh are Britons."

Schroeder nodded, "Are they? I guess they are. Yet somehow I think that would not be their first choice of self-identification or allegiance."

"For someone who professes no interest in politics you seem particularly well versed and thoughtful."

"Given that those struggles are centuries old, it is hard not to know about them. And I have put my foot in it several times equating all Britons as Englishmen. An American misconception I can assure you. But I only know the details enough to avoid embarrassment, I take no side. Still, I've come all this way, I might as well hear you out."

And Churchill looked over Schroeder's shoulder and waved toward the manor house. Presently a young man trotted down the grassy sward towards the fish pond and the two men.

He was dressed in a business suit of an older fashion, but with no insignia or other identifying mark. The wet grass made his shoes glisten. He bowed slightly from the neck upon arrival.

"Jeremy, bring the papers we talked about into the dining room. Professor Schroeder will be joining us for lunch. And have your maps and photos ready for him in the library. Thank you." Jeremy nodded and turned to go.

"And you Mr. Schroeder must, must, must take a vow to never divulge what I am about to tell you, as it is of the uttermost national importance and highest level of secrecy."

Schroeder nodded his assent.

"No sir, you must speak the vow aloud."

Schroeder's eyes narrowed but he spoke clearly, vowing never to divulge to anyone what he was about to hear.

"You can, after hearing this, refuse this commission and leave here having dismissed the entire interview from your memory. My contact tells me you are worthy of that trust."

Schroeder racked his brain for some clue as to who the informant might be, but he came up with nothing, save perhaps the Dean who after all, had encouraged him and loaned him his car. He made a mental note to find out if the Dean knew Churchill personally.

The two men repaired to the house where Churchill poured two dashes of scotch and indicated a seat for Schroeder.

"Lunch will be served presently," announced a member of the staff, who had entered the room and left it just as quickly, closing the double doors behind her.

"Let me give you something to stew on, during our meal. We will speak in detail later in the library."

Churchill explained that he was certain war with Germany was coming, given the recent capitulation of Prime Minister Neville Chamberlain to Nazi desires to annex the Sudetenland, a portion of Czechoslovakia, bordering on Germany. Churchill explained the Nazis would simply move their demands to engulf the whole country by referencing the chaos they themselves had created by splitting the country with their annexation. He expressed his belief that the entire country would succumb to the Germans within a year. And then other predominately German speaking areas would be under heavy German pressure to come under the Nazi yoke of 'protection'.

"Surely the Germans know they will be challenged if they do anything by force?"

"Perhaps, but I'll let you in on a little secret, many high ranking British officials including some in the Foreign Office, are Nazi sympathizers if not outright Nazis."

"And you mean to stop them?"

"The Nazis have been rearming Germany for years now in direct violation of the Treaty of Versailles. The French have bleated their concern but done nothing. They are particularly worried as their large military and long standing animosity with the Germans has put a target on their backs. After the trenches of the Great War, they want no part of any conflict, and make Neville's pacifism look downright hawkish."

"I hardly see that standing up to Hitler will make you look foolish to the Americans."

"It's not the standing up, it's the method. What I am talking about doing with you, is investigating a mere trifle, which could lead to a tiny strategic play in a much wider and deeper game. It might not bear any fruit, and yet the very act of thinking it and acting upon it, would look very desperate to our American friends."

"Perhaps looking desperate is in England's best interest."

Churchill looked at Schroeder silently for a moment over the top of his tilted glass of Scotch.

"Without going into a lot of detail, we need to acquire several keys, actual keys once in possession of the Royal families of Russia, Germany, Austria and Denmark, given as tokens of attachment by Queen Victoria to her daughters as each Princess was married off into the leading noble families of Europe."

Schroeder shook his head, "That certainly came out of nowhere."

Churchill was resigned, "I told you it was a shot in the dark."

"Do we know where these keys are and what they look like? All of these Royal Families are given to history now. Well, except Spain I suppose, but that is still an open question with their Civil War still undecided."

"There were five daughters of Victoria and Albert. Four of whom were married into noble families in Europe. All four of them eventually, either directly or through their offspring, produced Queens of various realms. We know where three of these keys are and we are actively searching for the fourth. We need you to visit these countries under the guise of academic research and request those keys, among other artifacts to bring back for study. With war looming, now is the time to retrieve them while it is still a relatively easy thing to do."

"Retrieve them? What are these keys? What if I cannot get them?"

Churchill sighed. He took a deep sip of scotch and swirled it momentarily in his mouth. He pulled on his cigar, and then leaned back in his chair, slowly expelling the smoke.

"Queen Victoria had a large family. She sent four of her daughters to marry into the Royal Families of Europe. Upon their weddings Victoria gifted each daughter with an ornate key, saying it was the key to her British heart, and an entry way back home should she need it. All very symbolic and romantic you know. But they are more than that. We need these keys. They open a vault at Windsor Castle."

"And what is inside?"

"We do not know. But legend suggests forcing the box will destroy its contents. And what is allegedly in the box could have some bearing on our future fight with Germany. The vault is disguised, it is really quite small and hidden in plain sight. It is a safe if you will."

"And these contents are vital and will help Britain in a war?"

"Presumably, or I wouldn't be interested in them, would I?" said Churchill with a flash of anger. He took a deep breath, "Given our precarious defensive position we are certain that the possibility should be explored. We are woefully unprepared for a serious conflict. One doesn't want to leave any stone unturned, only to regret it later."

"So why wasn't this done prior to the Great War?"

"A good question. Perhaps people at the time did not consider the situation as dire. Then there was little concern that Great Britain would be invaded."

"And why does such a mission come from you Sir Winston, who currently holds no position in cabinet nor any government post, save your seat in parliament?"

"Ah, the American in you has arrived. And the American in me will answer. Our own government, and through them, the Foreign Office, have been quite pacifist regarding Hitler. That is no secret. They do not consider his ambitions to be more than the natural restoration of Germany in the wake of the Treaty of Versailles. They are wrong. I have been orchestrating an extensive intelligence operation from right here, and fairly openly, so I can collect and present facts to the government, facts which they appear to be willfully ignoring. Going around the official bureaucracy and those directing it, is my attempt to underline the significance of events and to embarrass our government into taking necessary action to prepare for the inevitable war. I hope also to expose the Nazi sympathizers in the Foreign Office. Frankly I am surprised Chamberlain has not called me out on this and tried to shut me down. Many high ranking government officials are quietly involved. England is so far behind in preparations it is likely we will never catch up and will require our American cousins to intervene. If we were invaded tomorrow we would be fighting with sticks and stones.

"When I say we want the keys, Chamberlain has no idea about this. It's another way to insulate the government should this go sideways. The 'we' I refer to is myself and Princess Elizabeth who first approached me a few months ago with the legend and knowledge of this vault and its probable importance. She is privy to things that the rest of us will never know. I have agreed to help her."

"Princess Elizabeth? She is just a young girl. Does the King know anything about this?"

"He told her the story of the vault a few years ago but he does not know that she recently approached me. I suspect that her mother, the Queen, is advising her. We both thought it better that her father did not know, should things go poorly. Plausible denial and all that, you know. And do not underestimate the young Princess. She is very quick to cut through the details."

"So what do you want from me?"

"You can travel to Europe as part of your study of Victorian Era society, get the keys and bring them back. It is our understanding that the keys themselves are known about in these capitals but they are thought of only as wedding presents, trifles and items for museum display. They are fairly ornate."

Churchill explained that the artifacts attached to Queen Victoria's daughters that were in Germany and in Spain, were in museums. Permission had been granted to the Foreign Office to send a qualified academic to study these artifacts and others like them. Any transport of artifacts would be considered upon a more detailed request. Denmark was quite willing to loan the artifacts to England. Only Russia had demurred, claiming they had no knowledge of any British artifacts attached to Alice Maud Mary, the mother of Alexandria who married Nicholas II the last Romanov czar. Further official requests had not been made to avoid drawing too much attention to the artifacts. British agents were subtly looking for them in museums or in official correspondence to try to track down their location.

"So you would be correct that this mission is more than just an academic exercise."

The two men were summoned to the dining room and Churchill directed his guest to sit.

Luncheon was served and heartily enjoyed without another word said on the matters at hand. Discussion turned to the University and Churchill's connections there. Probing a little, nothing leaped out at Schroeder regarding a possible person who may have recommended him to Churchill.

After a round of drinks and some banter including a few inquiries regarding any mutual acquaintances, Churchill directed Schroeder to his study. There, maps were strewn over anything even close to a flat surface. The men scoured a map of Vienna, noting the University and the national museum. Churchill suggested a tour of these museums would begin in Austria to get a sense of the German occupation and to broaden the research aspect of the trip to a place without a Victorian key.

"They will suspect you are observing for us. It would not be out on line to give them something to suggest it to deflect from your real objective."

The two men looked closely at a map of central Berlin and again noted the university location.

"Remember this is a research trip first for a book you are writing."

Schroeder leaned back in his chair, ramrod straight. His eyes blinked.

"When would I go?"

"Next week to Austria to set the ground work for your travel and study. Then to Spain and afterwards to Berlin and Russia."

Churchill produced a key, holding it up and twisting it gently so it glinted in the light.

"They look like this, though they all have a slightly different design, usually with appropriate symbols either formed in the metal or created by judicious use of precious stones. The symbols are not entirely obvious as the Princesses generally married Prince's of German landed nobles whose familial lands were later subsumed into a Greater Germany by Bismarck. In all instances it is the daughters of these original seeds planted by Victoria that reached the Royal House. For example Princess Beatrice Mary Victoria married a Prince of Battersburg and their daughter Victoria married into the Spanish Royal Family. And Princess Victoria Adelaide Mary Louise was the mother of German Emperor Friedrich Wilhelm II, after she married into the Prussian Royal Family. I'm pretty good at remembering all of this, what?"

"It must be very important. So that is the key for Denmark?" Schroeder said indicating the key Churchill still held.

"Yes. We want you to study the keys, photograph them quite openly along with other artifacts as they present themselves. If you cannot convince authorities to let you take it among other artifacts you want to study, you need to either spirit it away or take a pressing and make a detailed drawing along with a photograph, paying particular attention to the business end of the key. The drawing can be done openly and perhaps without exacting dimensional detail, again to throw them off the track. However, the pressing should be done subtly, unknown to your hosts if possible. And with the highest level of exacting detail. Of course the keys are our focus but you have to study everything Victoria gave her children when she married them off. And broaden your investigations to other noble marriages for comparison sake. We don't want Hitler knowing exactly what we are interested in. In fact we are sending a few other academics to study other aspects of Continental history as it pertains to Britain, to further hide our true purpose."

"Well that's comforting I suppose."

Churchill pulled open a desk drawer and took out a small box. In the box was a five inch long block of a firm but malleable modeling clay, about three inches wide and one high. Churchill took the key and pressed its narrow stem flat into the malleable block. He took a book and applied pressure evenly to it. The task completed he flicked the key loose by the top of its handle loop which he had left slightly overhanging the edge of the block.

"Voila. Box it and stick it in your pocket and you have completed your task."

"I need to think on this. I am not a spy, and in fact get quite nervous when I'm out of my element."

"That's the beauty of this. You are right in your element. And while removing the keys is a better outcome, the moulds will do as we can fashion our own version from the impressions you make.

"You have three days to decide or I will have to find someone else. And the best part, for you? I guarantee your paper and/or eventual book on Queen Victoria's wedding presents will find lucrative publication. I have some pull with publishers."

# Chapter Three

Schroeder sat in his small campus office ruminating about his visit to Chartwell. His eyes blankly scanned the shelves for books but he was thinking not seeing.

He had begun to consider the gold fish that so fascinated Churchill, thinking that they swam endlessly around the pond, searching for who knows what. He wondered if the fish recognized their starting point and knew that theirs was a small world, or if every turn in the pond seemed new to them, creating an infinite world view. A knock at his door interrupted his reverie.

"Come."

The door opened and there stood his Dean, Arthur Cadswell, MA PhD, a man who knew more about King Arthur than perhaps even Merlin himself.

"I should thank you for the loan of the car. I parked it where you asked and left the keys under the seat."

"Yes, yes. So what was the purpose of the summons?"

Schroeder hadn't entirely thought through the events of the previous day so he held back.

"Churchill knows I am an American and he wanted to feel me out about the American attitude to Hitler and Chamberlain and Europe."

"How would you know? You haven't been to America in 10 years."

"That's what I told him. I do however, regularly correspond with old colleagues and I sit for a pint now and again with a few old friends who've taken the same career path that I have. What is perhaps strange, is that he knew all that."

"Well, you can't fault old Winston for trying. He's been a thorn in Neville's side since Baldwin retired and elevated Chamberlain to PM."

"Nice countryside down there. Lovely rolling hills, dotted here and there with old homes, large buildings and small towns. You should take a ride down there sometime."

"Well old man, most of England is like that outside the cities. You really should get out of London more often. The wife prefers the Cotswold Hills - north-west of here. Same sort of thing, rolling hills, picturesque and all that, but without the pretense of Kent. Fewer manor houses, historic monuments and great piles of crumbling masonry. And more thatched roofs. Somehow leaky and moldy thatched roofs have a cachet that I do not understand."

"Well, thank you again for the car. Certainly convenient when you are traveling off the beaten track."

"Think nothing of it."

The two men shared a cup of tea and chatted briefly about the upcoming Christmas Break. The Break gave Schroeder an idea. He could plan a trip to the Continent then. He had no family ties or obligations, and the down time would be perfect. He would get brownie points from the Dean for taking on a new research project, especially if publication was in the offing. He decided to wait for a bit before suggesting it to Cadswell to avoid an easy association between the idea for a trip and his visit to Chartwell. He did send a note to Churchill suggesting the slight delay in the timing of his trip. He was hopeful that Churchill would see the delay of a few weeks as prudent under the circumstances.

A few days later, after an afternoon lecture and waiting out his proscribed afternoon office hours, Schroeder walked to a nearby pub. He preferred the Rose and Thistle as it was a little further from the University and tucked back into a few twisting streets of South Ealing, central London's nondescript western end. Ealing was out past Westminster, its picturesque and better known central west end. The historic medieval buildings of Westminster, the street layout, and of course the tourist haunts of Parliament, Big Ben, and the Abbey overshadowed Ealing in every way.

He sat at the bar and ordered a pint. The pub was mostly empty in the late afternoon, with the end of the working day rush soon to come.

The barmaid, familiar with her customer, plunked a shard of ice into the glass.

With a nod, Schroeder smiled at her in thanks. He wasn't sure it really made the beer much colder but it was a nice illusion that made the drink more palatable. He hadn't brought too many American quirks with him to Europe but a preference for cold beer was one of them.

He paid, preferring to not run a tab, and had taken only two sips when a gentleman in a gray suit slid in beside him. He hung his hat on the hook under the bar, ordered and took a few deep draughts before making himself known.

"I've been expecting you Anderson. I think we should move to a more isolated spot."

Anderson arched his eyebrows and made to stand up, carrying his glass to a table that Schroeder selected, deep in an alcove far from the bar and any foot traffic.

"Churchill thinks there will be war."

"Wow, such insight. I expect three quarters of Britain thinks there will be war. You couldn't tell me that at the bar?"

"He thinks Americans will side with Britain and he wants me to be his eyes and ears on campus and among the Americans I know. He knows about my connections to US intelligence. In fact, I expect we are being watched now." His companion remained placid but it took an effort. "He claims he has an extensive intelligence network operating right under the noses of the British Foreign Office, with some of the high ranking bureaucrats more beholden to him than they are to Chamberlain."

"It's not treason?"

"Oh, no, quite the opposite. He says that Chamberlain is so afraid of war he refuses to countenance it by making any preparations. As if taking the possibility seriously would cause it to come about. Churchill is laying the groundwork of eventual preparations. Chamberlain looks the other way as he can countenance preparations as long as those efforts are not official government policy."

"More?"

"No. I am to let him know shortly if I am on side with him."

Anderson took out a cigarette case and offered Schroeder one, though he knew that his companion did not smoke. He carefully put the case away into his breast pocket and used a match supplied with an ash tray that was already on the table.

"Give him an affirmative. We will have to work out a different way of exchanging information, if they are on to you. Leave it to me, I will contact you."

"We will still have to meet or they will think it odd. Perhaps they know about you too."

"Of course, you are right. By God old man, that's the first cloak and dagger thing you've ever said. We'll make a spy out of you yet."

"I'm not a spy, only an observer."

Anderson tipped his head, not entirely buying into Schroeder's assertion. The two men chatted briefly about the Kent countryside and the particulars of Chartwell, then finished their drinks and parted ways.

* * * * * * * * *

Churchill wrote back to Schroeder.

"Agreed. I will be in touch with details."

Churchill had a discussion with several European historians in various disciplines wanting them all to conduct their light espionage in belief that theirs was the true mission. They visited monuments, calculated crowds and tried to take a measure of the public mood in Nazi occupied Europe and in various other capitals. Churchill himself travelled to France to visit friends and relatives while keeping his own eyes and ears open.

Churchill explicitly told each one of his academic agents to do nothing that could be construed as spying. They were not to go out of their way, they were to avoid photography, especially as most of these trips were arranged as business meetings or academic research. Photographs of tourist haunts rarely led to any real intelligence. The travellers all thought he was concerned for their safety, but he could not afford an international incident that could be traced back to him. Chamberlain would be forced to deal with his operation if confronted about it publically.

Churchill received the reports from these travels and it was obvious that Europe was preparing for war. It was noticeable in the construction projects, it was in conversations with merchants, mothers, and farmers. Soldiers popped up in unlikely places, a convoy of trucks here, a group of soldiers on leave there. It was in the notes of resignation in the voices of millions. And yet, few understood how this conflict would play out. Many believed that Germany was merely gathering its ethnic progeny and would cease to be aggressive once that mission was accomplished.

Those thinking it would lead to war believed it would descend into the grinding, futile trench warfare of the Great War. They hid behind the size of the French army and its Maginot Line preparations. Most people, even the generals and official planners, expected the next war to mirror the last. A common and usually fatal determination.

A few others knew differently. Mechanization of the infantry was obvious even if the Nazis were trying to hide their true strength. One of his travellers had seen a long freight train south of Cologne hauling trucks with army insignia.

The size and scope of the air force, once an afterthought, made it now a forward offensive tactical branch of the military. The size of planes and their speed and reach had increased dramatically from the time of the Great War. Intelligence on the numbers of planes coming out of German factories, and advertisements looking for pilots, provided  additional detail on how the Nazis planned to utilize the air component. Flight improvements had essentially made airplanes an entirely different weapon than they had been. Then, small planes with one or two aboard were mostly forward observations posts. Now they could carry a substantial payload of bombs and travel at much higher speeds and longer distances.

Into this mix Christoph Schroeder found himself on a train from Paris, bound for Vienna at Christmas 1938. The Nazis had just convinced the Czechoslovakians to gift them the northern part of their nation, the Sudetenland, a heavily industrial area in the

Carpathian Mountains. Not only were mines for the raw material of iron and steel lost to the Nazis in the transfer of land, but the Mountains themselves offered a much easier defence against invasion. The Czechs were now laid bare to Nazi determinism.

The Nazis had already completed the annexation of Austria the previous spring, bringing their Germanic brethren under the wing of the Reich. Some Austrians applauded but most were uneasy with the change in control.

Schroeder's train passed through Bavaria with a stop at Munich. The Nazi presence was obvious and as they entered the Austrian Tyrol there were increasing indications of German control culminating in a flurry of swastika flags, uniformed men and staff cars at the station in Salzburg, where the train made a short stop. Schroeder became a little uneasy at the show of forceful control and was unsure if more would come.

Once in Vienna he had had no trouble with the guards who gazed on his travel papers and happily directed him to his hotel. He noticed one guard looking at him closely, keeping his head tilted to peruse the travel documents while raising his eyes but not his head to look at Schroeder.

Schroeder contacted the museum telling his guide that he had arrived and reminding him that his research was on tokens and effects brought to their marriages by various members of the nobility. He suggested something he wanted to see and photograph and asked for direction on things he may not be familiar with. His research was to include many 19th century marriages for a comparison purposes, not just those which included a British subject.

Churchill had sent him to Vienna partly to throw any questioners off the scent of the true mission and because there were several young British women from the lesser nobility who married into

Austrian society.

Wandering through the great museum he saw a display that looked as if it was undergoing a refit.

"Aye that was the display of the Austrian Crown Jewels which has gone for a cleaning while they build a new display for them."

The space was empty but given a slight discolouration of the velvet on which the artifacts had rested it was easy to see that a crown, scepter and some broaches had once rested there. Beside it were two mannequins displaying dresses and another with a full formal suit, complete with a sash and some subtle nods to a more military style of dress.

"They haven't taken everything?"

"They took the . . . easiest things to carry first. The rest will be removed shortly to allow the new work.

There have been some security concerns and museum officials want to ensure any new display area is sufficiently guarded and safe."

"Is it possible to see them?"

The guide shook his head, "I probably shouldn't say, as I am German, as are most Austrians, but I am not comfortable being ruled from Berlin. Hitler sent people in to take some of these artifacts before we knew we might have to protect them. I expect they are not coming back, no matter what the promises."

"Whatever could Berlin want with them?"

"Credibility. German rule does not seem natural. Vienna needs to remain in control of itself and should have more of a say. Our traditions are similar but different. Please forget all of that, I've said too much."

"Your countrymen appear to be pleased with the new regime, and were quick to welcome their cousins."

The guard nodded, "Yes, I suppose they did but Berlin seemed to take an unnatural joy in it, and completed it with such overbearing speed that it seemed less of our choice than we were given to believe. They did it before any opposition could get organized. The Nazis have cornered the Germanic tendency to be overbearing." He smiled ruefully.

Schroeder merely nodded. "I'll leave the disposition of the Crown Jewels to you, I am here to study the English influence on Austria, primarily through dress and design brought into the country by marriages of the nobility. I am looking to contrast the English approach with other Europeans in the same situation. I believe the Embassy and our Foreign Office made a formal request for some artifacts to be loaned briefly to us, the specifics to be determined upon my visit."

"Yes, that is so, however our Museum Director has declined that request. And yet, he was quite willing to allow you to study anything we have while you are here."

He looked about conspiratorially, "I think our Director is concerned about being accused by our new government of spiriting artifacts out of the country."

"How, unfortunate. What I am interested in is the social constructs of the tokens given and received in these society weddings. Not being able to borrow some things may necessitate my staying here for longer than I had intended. I trust photography is permitted?"

The guide nodded slightly in acknowledgement.

Christoph Schroeder spent several days in a variety of Austrian museums, and managed to get access to some of their collected documents which he studied and took notes. He quickly realized he would need actual notes and information to write any paper he might present to publishers at West London.

On the third day, he was at the Sisi Museum, famed for its collections of textiles, furniture and clothing. He was nestled over a letter that was particularly difficult to read as it was written in English cursive by an unpracticed hand.

He heard the tramp of heavy feet come up behind him, and glanced around to see four SS men led by an officer heading directly for him.

"Herr Schroeder, welcome to the Sisi Museum, I am at your service, Major Hans Kilhofer."

"Thank you for allowing me my research," said Schroeder in German, with a nod. "I hope I am not inconveniencing anyone here. I had hoped to stay only a few days and take a few trifles back to England with me for further study and professional photographs. I am writing a book on the subject of intermarriage between the nobility in Europe, particularly focussing on the 19th century. I see that some of the smaller pieces were made by the same jeweller."

"Yes, unfortunately the Museum Director is frightened to let anything out of his sight," Killhofer smiled. "Perhaps we could assist you with a professional photographer?"

"Wonderful, that would be most helpful. I would be happy to give the photographer a photo credit in my publication and perhaps organize with the publishers for a small honorarium upon publication."

The next day a small, nervous man arrived and introduced himself as the appointed photographer. He was well equipped with lights and lenses and a few measures of black cloth to use as backgrounds. At Schroeder's direction he took photos of documents, photos of artifacts and after two days presented the English professor with a sheaf of 8 x 10s with his name and address carefully spelt out on the envelope. Another day in the Museum and Schroeder would move to another before wrapping up his visit and moving on to Spain.

Late in the afternoon Schroeder was hunched over a document at the Museum when he heard the tramping of booted feet approach. He looked up to see Kilhofer only a few yards away with his usual escort of black uniformed SS.

"I trust you found the photographer helpful?"

"Yes, Major, and thank you so much for arranging for his services. I am hopeful my publisher will provide a payment."

"May I see the photos, I want to make sure he completed his work to the highest standard."

"Oh, you are a photographer yourself?"

Kilhofer smiled through his teeth. "I am familiar with quality."

Schroeder reached for the sheaf of photos and watched as Killhofer leafed through them, slowing down only when it became evident he wasn't considering the quality but rather the subject matter.

"Why are there so many photos of letters?"

"They are hard to read Herr Major. And many times the letters would have to be copied entirely as they are right on point with what I am studying. It is amazing how poor the handwriting was of these privileged people; or perhaps not."

Kilhofer handed the sheaf back, pronouncing the photos very good.

"I will be visiting Kaiserliche Schatzkammer Wien and the Kunsthistorisches Museum. Is it possible for the photographer to spend a few hours with me in each location?"

Hilhofer made a pretense of considering the request before loaning out the man's services. He did not consult the photographer.

Schroeder found himself on occasion lost in his research as he found untold examples of wealth and ostentation among the nobility, who were consumed with trying to outdo each other or make impressions upon each other they deemed necessary to maintain the social strata and their place in it.

Kilhofer paid him a visit just before he left the country.

"Your last day in Austria, Herr Schroeder?"

"Yes, I have collected quite a large amount of information on the subject. I have quite the task in front of me deciphering it all."

"Will you be returning to England?"

"Yes, but first I am to go to Spain, and then on to Berlin."

Kilhofer smiled, "Berlin museums are the finest."

"If they are, I will have more detail than I can possibly use, but I don't want to miss anything. I am looking for detail and do not want to gloss over anything."

"I hope you have not missed anything. If so, perhaps I will have the pleasure of seeing you again."

"Again, thank you for your help Herr Major."

Kilhofer excused himself but sent two SS men to help Schroeder with his things as he boarded the train which would get him first to Barcelona and eventually to Madrid.

# Chapter Four - December 1938

Spain was embroiled in civil war. Once across the Pyrenees the train was boarded by government security forces. They were there to guard the train but took the time to search out contraband and scrutinize the passengers. The Royalist Republican government was anxious to accommodate an envoy from Britain whose mission was academic, sentimental and sympathetic to the Royal Family.

Queen Victoria's granddaughter, herself named Victoria had married into the Spanish Royal family during the turbulent later half of the 19th century when Spain was trying to establish a constitutional monarchy.

Schroeder arrived in Madrid as the Nationalist rebels were beginning to turn the tide against superior numbers and munitions controlled by the Republican side. Barcelona was under imminent threat of falling to the Nationalists. He met with various officials to outline his plans and received a warm welcome. He was led into a room in a Madrid museum, to get started on his research, when he immediately saw the key.

It was among a group of personal effects of the Princess, tamped onto a display board that held various pieces of jewelry.

Oversized, it was about eight inches in length, with an ornate loop of several inlayed pieces of reflective semi-precious stones forming the handle, shaped into a traditional heart. The larger reflective stones had a slightly yellow hue and Schroeder expected they were amethyst. The business end of the key was burnished silver in appearance but showed no signs of oxidation. Either the Spanish were fastidious in their maintenance of even the smallest items in their museums or the key was not made of silver, thought Schroeder.

He made the usual rounds of photographs and document research but there was little at hand on the life of Victoria Battenburg.

Schroeder's request to remove several pieces to take with him for further study produced a quizzical look from his attendant. However the next day he was summoned into a meeting with the museum director and a stout, well dressed man, who identified himself as a high ranking bureaucrat in the Foreign Ministry.

"I understand you have been inquiring about a number of small artifacts attached to Princess Victoria. We always assumed she was of German extraction as she came to us through her father Prince Harold of Battenburg?"

"Aye, Prince Harry was her father, but Princess Beatrice Mary, daughter of our Queen Victoria, was her mother, making Victoria her grandmother. The social mores of the time were so interesting don't you think?"

The bureaucrat harrumphed, "Er, ah, I suppose, Herr Schroeder, but it is that sort of thing that has so inflamed the Nationalists here in Espana."

"Please do not be confused, I am Mister Schroeder, or preferably

Professor Schroeder, as I am an American, though, with my German name it is easy to be confused."

"Well, I was unsure as you have come from Britain."

"Yes, I have lectured at the University of West London for several years now. They are far more interested in the doings of the nobility than are Americans."

The bureaucrat pursed his lips, "We have considered your request to borrow the artifacts. Given our situation here, we would like you to take all of these artifacts to England until our troubles have been sorted out. The Ministry and the Museum do not believe they are safe should the Nationalists . . . strengthen."

Schroeder quickly made some inquires through the British Embassy and several large trunks were loaded for travel back to Britain with him, the key among the treasures.

Officially neutral, Britain leaned to the Republican side, and a restoration of the democratic government opposed by much of the Spanish military on the Nationalist side. The Germans were actively supporting the Nationalists in part to oppose the communist leaning Republicans. As is the case in most of these civil conflicts, it is never easy to pin down the motives of each side, as each was an amalgam of similar but competing interests, joined together by convenience and ultimately their particular preferred brand of public administration.

There seemed to be an ever present threat that the Germans would join in the war in force, which kept the vastly superior Republican forces from sweeping the Nationalists aside, as if doing so, would invite a large German force to intervene. The Nazis were on hand as advisors and likely forward observers. They did loan some weaponry and a few officers to help organize Nationalist forces but they were content to remain a threat rather than a potent force on the ground. They had other concerns in Europe.

Professor Schroeder made the usual round of museums, examined documents and taking photos of things that he would not bring back to England.

* * * * * * * * * *

Upon his return to Britain Schroeder met with Churchill. This time he was met at Victoria Station by a car sent for him and quickly driven to Chartwell. Churchill was again sitting by his fish pond. He looked up from his pondering at the sight of Schroeder striding down the grassy bank toward the pond.

"You never know when snow will come to Kent. British weather being what it is, a lovely crisp winter day can quickly change into ice and snow and leave the countryside peaceful in its aftermath but impassable. And two days later it melts."

"It was much nicer in Spain. Well sunnier I guess, but everyone I spoke to is frigid with fear that the rebels will win. I expect you heard of our windfall?"

"I did. Sometimes fortune falls in your lap."

"I hardly knew there was any conflict there, but I was officially steered away from it. I will say there is an undercurrent of tension in that country, the officials I spoke to are suspicious of everybody and everything. The government's official sympathy with Russia is only deep enough to be noticed, but it's as if they fear getting too close. And Germany is nowhere, but everywhere in the air. Fear of what the conflict could become if the Germans enter in numbers pervades every conversation."

"Both the communists and the fascists have a history of seizing control. A government which embraces a more moderate and malleable approach to its issues, is sure to shy away from either."

"That's the first time I've ever heard revolutionaries described as moderates."

Churchill shrugged, "In this case there are other actors rather than just the civil combatants. No two wars are the same. One has to divorce one's self from ideology and expectations and deal with reality on the ground. It appears as if the rebels will capture Barcelona shortly. If that happens the Royalists will be hard pressed to turn the tide."

"You heard we have the key among the artifacts the Spanish put into our safe keeping?"

"Yes, and no. We do not have the key. The British bureaucracy now has the key, and it is documented, catalogued and enumerated in unimaginable ways. They take their guardianship seriously. Never underestimate the ability of a British bureaucrat to thwart your plans. It may be difficult to prise it from its vault. Though I am working on it."

Schroeder looked wounded. Churchill saw the disappointment and assured Schroeder that his mission was a success even if there was more work to be done.

"And now for the more difficult portion of your mission. Your successes in Austria and Spain have paved your path. And Denmark's co-operation helps as well. The Foreign Office has secured your travel to Berlin first, as your arrival from Russia might provoke extra scrutiny. You will go to Russia after your business in Berlin is complete but you will travel through Denmark and Sweden, making courtesy stops at museums in those places to cover your tracks. The Germans are suspicious of the Russians."

"Inquires on the matter have been well received?"

"Indeed, oddly so. I expect both governments are trying to preserve some thread of good will, especially as it costs them nothing, and this research project appears to be benign. However, I imagine they will both think you are engaged in a larger spy operation."

"I do not like the sound of that."

"Just play it straight, you are researching a book on social mores, and no harm should befall you. Do nothing suspicious and they will not suspect you. On second thought, they will always suspect you, but give them nothing to further that suspicion."

"Ah my, Sir Winston, you have a way of easing my fears and escalating my concerns at the same time. I am simply not cut out for this."

The trips were delayed a few weeks to soften the edge of any urgency the British might have tipped. When the Nazis completed their annexation of Czechoslovakia in March, Churchill was beside himself for waiting. The British and the French stood by, unwilling to take a stand and hopeful that the Nazis had completed their territorial ambitions. Chamberlain's policy of appeasement had reached its zenith even though factions in the British government sought to extend it. Officially they were determined to avoid the horrors of the trenches which had concluded only 20 years before.

Tensions were increasing as the spring of 1939 deepened. Schroeder travelled to Berlin.

"Remember Schroeder there will be war. Hitler cannot help himself as he has not faced any serious opposition, as the French dither and we remain pacifist. It is that stance that is inviting a blood bath, the second in less than a complete generation, though Neville believes otherwise. Unfortunately former Mayors do not understand power vacuums or the Teutonic mind."

"And you do?"

"Aye, remember young buck that I was in the thick of it in India, South Africa and during the Great War. Pacifist intensions thwarted our plans in those places too. One must have an iron will to defeat the bloody minded. You can only have peace if you are willing and able to wage war. Hitler is testing that assertion all across Europe."

* * * * * * * * * *

Arrival in Berlin provided an insight into Hitler's purpose. Construction projects abounded in the core of the city, however, most of the building involved the destruction of old medieval streets and passageways and the construction of a wide east-west thoroughfare through the center of the city. A project that was well underway.

Herr Hitler had a wide ranging vision for Germany. From lebensraum and territorial ambitions, to reuniting the Saxon, Teutons and Aryans, to suppressing and eliminating unwanted peoples, it also included a reimagining of Germany down to its buildings and public spaces. Berlin was transforming from a regional, provincial capital into Germania, the focus of the new Greater Germany, and ultimately the power center of Europe.

The museum in Berlin which housed all the items of interest to Schroeder was closed but he was given a  guide and special access. He explained his academic interest to a dozen officials before being led to the displays. He photographed and catalogued everything. He looked at the key closely for a minute, commenting on its design and the precious gems embedded in the handle loop.

During his examination of two dresses which were owned by the princess, his guide was called out of the room.

"I have a request to attend to. I trust you have everything you need for about 30 minutes? I will return then and your next items of study can be fetched."

The attendant gone, Schroeder thought seriously of simply pocketing the key, but he feared being found out.  He wondered if he was being watched. The museum curator seemed deeply suspicious of him and would likely check that all the items remained. Once the attendant had left, Schroeder quickly pulled out the box containing the soft clay mould and he pressed the key into it. He heard a rustling by the door.

Fear, made him tuck the box in his jacket, the key still in the mould. His heart pounding and only silence coming from the door, he withdrew the box, removed the key and turned the mould over. Fearing he had not done the job properly he reapplied the key to the material, pressing down as much as possible without distorting the image being created. He removed the key and replaced it in the display, putting the box in his jacket pocket.

Breathing a sigh, he began to photograph several pages of notes detailing the dresses and jewelry. The door handle to the room jiggled, and opened slightly before the curator came back in.

"I trust you have everything you need?"

"I do but would like to see the next display of items you have. Some of the jewelry is exquisite but I am unable to identify the material that it is made from. Is it white gold?"

"Most of it is white gold, some is silver. Among the other pieces, especially the smaller ones, some are made of platinum. The jewels themselves appear to be cut in Italy and Germany prior to being set in the pieces."

"Ah, I must check to see if they were fashioned in their country of origin or if the work was commissioned to the finest jewelers in Europe."

Schroeder completed his trip by leaving Germany through Denmark and mentioning that he was going on to Sweden where there were similar Royal connections.

As he sat on the train Schroeder was acutely aware of everything going on around him. He tried to remain placid. People he suspected were watching him were among the other passengers but he could not be certain. His nervous manner made his observers think he was a false spy, a faker designed to get them off their games.

"The British are tricky," said one. "This man is no more a spy than my mother, who looks guilty when she buys an expensive cut of meat."

"Or he is putting on the act to lull us, and he is really a super spy," said the other. They both laughed. "Seems a waste of time to watch him but I'm getting paid. Perhaps we should approach him and scare him a bit. If he is a spy it won't matter, if he isn't, we might have a bit of fun."

"Do it if you want, but he apparently studies dresses and jewelry of the nobility. And for that he gets paid well and is a respected member of academia."

"I think I missed my calling."

"So you like dresses too, Hans?"

Hans nearly choked. "No, no, I mean academia. Being paid to study useless things seems like an easy life. You know, first class travel, apparent respect inside the club . . . "

"That's a club I'd rather not be a member of." Both men smirked.

Schroeder passed the frontier with only a cursory check of his papers and an explanation that he was taking a few days in Copenhagen and then a ferry to Sweden.

A few days in Sweden scouring universities and museums, taking notes and photographs and he took a ship for Leningrad, formerly St. Petersburg, situated at the eastern end of the Baltic Sea.

"So you've been to Germany?" the border guard asked looking at his passport.

"I've been many places on my research trip. Leningrad is the last one. Then I must assemble my notes and complete the manuscript which my publishers are waiting for."

"You are to wait here for the guide who has been assigned to you."

\* \* \* \* \* \* \* \* \* \*

Leningrad was still in the grip of winter as March slipped into April. Snow was piled high but the sun would melt it a bit more each day, leaving rivulets of water during the day and ice at night at the base of the snow mounds.

The displays Schroeder was interested in, were at The Hermitage State Museum, a stunning piece of architecture on its own. Schroeder was awed and said so.

"Yes, Herr Schroeder, it is lovely. The Museum is housed in six buildings which make up the complex. The things you are most interested in are displayed in the Small Hermitage Building. I can arrange for you to tour the larger buildings if you wish."

"Yes, thank you, I would like to take that tour. However, please, I am a British-American and prefer to be addressed as Mister or Professor due to my academic rank."

"As you wish, Herr, er, Mister Schroeder. Many here do not trust Germans. So I am gratified to hear you are not one of them, despite your name. Does seeing the former Winter Palace help you to understand our revolution?"

"Perhaps, but I understood The Winter Palace had been trans-formed into a museum decades before the revolution."

"It was, but it was greatly expanded as much of the excess wealth of the nobility was nationalized. The grandeur of the buildings contrasted with the plight of everyday Russians. Hungry people do not make such minor distinctions when they clamour to feed their children."

"My family emigrated several generations ago to Pennsylvania and were farmers and then trades people. One of my aunts was Russian. I have heard some stories."

The guide smiled an oily smile through lips pulled back tightly to his face. Schroeder did not want to own up to the fact his aunt's family had escaped the Bolshevik revolution and had been minor landed nobility prior to their emigration. The guide appeared to suspect it but remained silent. The lower classes had little in the way of resources to leave the country.

During a quick tour of the Hermitage they settled on a few rooms of displays showing the decadence of the late Romanov period.

"Your interest in these items is to show the contrast between the nobility and the common peasants?"

"Yes, and how similar the nobility was to each other, even those from different countries. Oh, make no mistake, the British have significant issues with their class system. The Great War did much to level that playing field, but class divisions did not end. Some British, even those at the bottom of society, like their social customs for a number of reasons. As long as the upper classes don't impinge on their freedoms, the great mass of British are unconcerned with the heritage of the nobility."

"As you might expect we here in Soviet Russia frown on those divisions."

"It is interesting to me how the upper classes of all European countries acted toward each other and their own countrymen. In some respects the nobility chummed around with each other, no matter their national origin and thought themselves much different than their own working class countrymen. In many places they were expected to live much more formally that the average citizen to accentuate the differences in class. Some saw that as a burden and escaped to the Continent or America where they were

48

unknown."

"Though they might escape their apparent burden, they would not renounce it. It was the fruits of that burden which enabled their escape."

Schroeder nodded. "I guess having a title could come in handy in certain situations." He himself was an historian, not a monarchist nor a republican, though his American roots gave him an air of detachment.

The display was entirely of items owned by the Czarina Alexandria. He dutifully photographed and catalogued them, having the accompanying written details of each item translated for him.

Asking after items owned by her mother, he was taken into the cellars of the museum and provided with several boxes. The key was among them.

When his guide moved to a shelf to get another box Schroeder impulsively took the key and slipped it into his jacket's inside breast pocket.

He tried to forget about it but was consumed with the idea that the key caused a strange bulge in his lapel. He hunched over to conceal it. And he forced himself to look into box after box of other items, even after the box that had contained the key was replaced on the shelf, his larceny apparently unnoticed.

He fought the urge to finish his research and get out of Russia. He knew he had to complete his task for appearances and to have the necessary material to complete his book on the matter.

"I will require another day to go through these items as the photography takes more time than I thought."

"As you wish. I can escort you to your hotel and arrange for you to be delivered here in the morning."

"I should like to wander about the city after dinner and have a bit of a look around."

"I will arrange to have a guide escort you."

"No, that's quite alright."

"You will get more out of your wanderings if you know what you are looking at."

Sensing he was not going to be allowed free access, Schroeder acquiesced. He took some time to freshen up, thinking on how to arrange his notes and photo reels so they would not be disturbed as he fully believed his room would be searched when he was gone.

He decided to take a pressing of the key and leave it in its box in his room with boxes containing several other pressings. The key itself, he took with him, this time carefully sewn into the lining of his jacket, just under his less used left arm.

Leaving the hotel he suggested they just walk about and then perhaps take a taxi to see a few more distant sights. Spring was in full bloom in Britain but in the much more northerly St. Petersburg it was only just creeping closer and the daylight was not yet able to keep the city illuminated as long as he might have wanted to wander.

Directing him Schroeder felt the guide patting him on the back to direct his movements, from the elevator, through the hotel's side entrance doors and again on the street, in the direction of the Neva River. He wandered about and chatted, and the guide enquired deeply about what he had seen both in Leningrad and in other capitals, how it impacted his research and what his next project might be.

They took an hour at the fabled Catharine Palace just outside the city. The façade looked like the Palace of Versailles near Paris, and several drawing rooms were decorated in much the same way. His guide led him through the palace stopping briefly in the Amber Room, a mid-sized drawing room where the walls were decorated entirely in amber, giving the room a golden glow richer and deeper than even the real gold accents in the room.

Architecture was not Schroeder specialty but he could not help but be impressed. His guide used the time to probe his thinking with open ended questions. They were penetrating but Schroeder played up his disinterest in Germany, in Hitler and leaned on his time in academic pursuits.

The next day he resumed his time at the museum. After lunch his guide was changed. This time it was a thin man with a small scar to the side of his left eye. He introduced himself as Alexi. He was small of stature, though not out of line with most Russians that Schroeder had encountered. He appeared to be about 40 years old but involuntarily exhibited the dexterity of a man much younger, gracefully reaching for boxes, and lifting heavy items easily.

They made small talk and the new guide enquired about the helpfulness of the old one.

"Mister Schroeder I understand you have a Russian aunt? Would you be interested in doing her a service?"

Schroeder was completely caught off guard. "I suppose, but I do not know her terribly well. She was the bride of my father's younger brother, a man engaged in the agricultural machinery business in and around Eastern Pennsylvania."

"We have taken the liberty of researching your aunt, Libnia Molotov, both before she left Russia and after she emigrated with her family. The family left considerable property in Russia though much of it was destroyed in the troubles. We would like to restore some of the lands to her, if you would help us."

"I can certainly let her know. Who would she contact?"

"Oh, no, we can contact her. In return we would like to have her observations and yours as well."

At first Schroeder did not understand, but slowly the real object of the Soviet's desire became clearer.

"We would like you to help us understand her life in Pennsylvania, the way of living, the methods of farming and the like."

"You would have to ask her. I'm afraid I am not a farmer."

"We are trying to understand the high levels of productivity in America. Is it the land? The methods? The workers? The machines?"

Schroeder saw no harm in talking about these subjects. But the Soviet wanted more.

"And what about England, how do farms there differ from Pennsylvania?"

"I'm no expert in agriculture. I have spent no time on farms, especially in Britain. Surely you could find this information out from various resource books and perhaps a question or two of your contacts in America or England."

"That's what you are Mr. Schroeder. Do you have any plans to go back to America, even for a visit?"

Schroeder nodded explaining he was likely to make a visit to his family at Christmas, some eight months in the future. He did not mention that he feared war and the likelihood that travel would be cut off.

"Perhaps when you are there you could deliver the good news about the land to your aunt?"

"Okay, what should I tell her?"

The official gave him a card with contact information and a description of three properties the Russian government had determined belonged to her family. He told Schroeder to have her to make contact if she wanted more information about the return of her family land. A Russian consular official would contact her at that time.

"Do you think there will be war, Mr. Schroeder?"

Uncomfortable, Schroeder answered in the affirmative.

"Perhaps you would be so kind as to speak to us of the English mood on the subject.

He was already an observer for the United States, on a mission for the British, entrusted by the Spanish royalists with their artifacts, considered friendly by heritage to the Germans and now he was being courted by the Russians.

Schroeder launched into a lengthy observation about British pacifism, a streak of Anglo-Saxon stubbornness and pride and a love of natural justice within the determination to keep rules and officials at arm's length.

"The British imbued their American offspring with the same determination to never be told what to do. The Americans applied that lesson back upon their own cousins in their Revolution. They both are stubborn and once their minds are made up, it is difficult to change them."

The Russian looked deeply at Schroeder taking in his thoughts, and making comments designed to elicit more information and perhaps build a little trust.

"And right now the British at least, are waging war against themselves, with a determination to stay out of Continental affairs, while fighting a competing understanding in some quarters, that they must intervene to maintain the status quo."

Returning to his hotel room, it was subtly evident that his room and belongings had been searched. items were carefully returned to where they had been prior to a search, but there was a touch of change  which tipped it off.

He was glad that he had taken casts of a few broaches in addition to the key or his interest in just that one artifact might have become known.

He feared the Russians would search the Museum for the artifacts in question and once they could not find the key their suspicions would escalate. He cursed himself for leaving the cast in his room.

A slow knock came to his door. He was petrified but he had to answer.

"Professor Schroeder?" The man, dressed like a hotel porter, spoke French without an Russian accent.

"Yes. Can I help you?"

"No, but perhaps I can help you. May I come in? No, on second thought let's go for a short walk outside the hotel, I'd like to point out a few sites. St. Petersburg is lovely this time of year - even for foreigners."

Schroeder froze momentarily, the key phrase Churchill had told him to look out for was not included.

"London is lovely too, spring comes earlier there," he returned.

"It's all about your expectations. Just wear a coat. Preparation is the key."

There it was, he thought, the final phrase matched the code he expected.

As they left the building the man at the front desk noticed them and after hesitating, lifted a phone receiver and made a quick call.

Schroeder and the man exited the hotel and started walking quickly towards the river. Schroeder lagged back unsure of himself. "Hurry, they will have seen us leave and a guide will catch us shortly. I am here to help you. Tell them you asked me to show you directions."

Schroeder scrambled to keep up.

"They are on to your possession. Give it to me and I will give it back to you on ship tomorrow. Quickly before they see us together. I work for Winston. Preparation is the key."

Hearing the signal phrase again, Schroeder acquiesced. It's sewn into my jacket."

"Damn it. Okay, go back to the hotel, say you went out for a bit of fresh air but that it is getting too dark to see much of anything. You haven't been away for more than two minutes. I will come to your room with breakfast and you can give me the key then. I would guess that they will search your luggage and affects when you board ship tomorrow. I will be on ship and will keep it until we land in Edinburgh. They may attempt to engage you on the voyage."

Schroeder nodded meekly.

"Go, the less time you are out of their sight the less suspicion there will be."

Schroeder turned to go back to the hotel, and after a few steps took a backward glance, only to see the man dressed as a porter had vanished. He was met by Alexi in the hotel lobby.

"Ah, Mr. Schroeder, back so soon?"

I wanted a bit of air and a look around. But you are right, I had no idea where to go to see anything. So I came back. I would like to take a stroll along the riverside before I go."

"There may not be time for that sir, your ship boards tomorrow morning. I trust you have all your notes ready for the voyage?"

Schroeder spent an uneasy night, fully expecting a knock on his door or worse. The next day, Schroeder called down for room service breakfast. When the knock came, he nearly jumped out of his chair. A porter wheeled in a tray with breakfast. It was not the same man with whom he had spoken the night before.

"Your breakfast is served sir. How do we deliver it so fast? Preparation is the key." The man put his finger to his lips and then his hands to his ears.

Schroeder withdrew the ornate key from his jacket and handed it to the porter thanking him for the early breakfast. He was a touch reluctant to hand it over but the code phrase was proper and the depth of relief he felt at no longer holding the artifact, more than compensated. After all, he still had the clay mould. He had checked for it once he had finished breakfast and found it untouched. He included it and a few other pressings with his research papers and photographs. Schroeder left the hotel, heading for the ship, accompanied by Alexi, the same guide who had shown him around the museums. He was asked to wait in a separate room while his papers and luggage were all thoroughly processed. Assured everything was in order he was escorted to the ship bound for Edinburgh.

The key, never far from his thoughts, was now out of his hands. He wondered who and how they would deliver it to him in Edinburgh, especially now that he was under surveillance.

\* \* \* \* \* \* \* \* \* \*

Having passed inspection he stood in the queue to board. Stepping past the guard whose attention was now fixed on the next person in line, he was anything but calm. Apparently okayed for boarding, he expected a tap on his shoulder at any time, but wasn't sure if it would be friendly or not. The ship was scheduled to make the three day journey to Edinburgh via Stockholm and Copenhagen.

Schroeder was on edge, nervous that anyone who appeared to be moving in his direction would collar him and ask uncomfortable questions. At first he stayed in his cabin but then fear that he would be accosted in his cabin alone and without witnesses forced him to wander the ship, believing that any confrontation would be better in public. He took to the deck, reading in a lounge chair or standing by the rail watching the sea, despite the cool spring air. He had to keep reminding himself that he held nothing incriminating, save perhaps the clay mould of the key, though with other clay moulds, the only thing unusual about that was that the key was missing from the museum.

"Why would I take the mould if I had the key?" he asked himself, trying to come up with an answer to a potential question.

The spring sun was warm on the deck but the sea breeze cool, almost cold. A few people stood near him as he gazed out to sea but none approached. Most people were wearing coats, which could easily conceal a weapon, he thought. Most had the coat open due to the sun. He worried about those with their coats done up.

The ship made a stop in Stockholm, trading passengers and some cargo. And after another day at sea he was beginning to feel as if he'd accomplished his mission as the ship navigated the entrance to the Baltic Sea near Copenhagen. A small launch caught up to the larger ship and two people came aboard, carrying several large sacks.

Most of the travellers did not see the event but Schroeder was on deck at the time and was concerned enough to ask someone near him what the small boat was doing.

"It's a mail drop. Mail from Russia to Denmark and mail from Russia and Denmark to Scotland and ultimately England," he was told.

The next day, out in the middle of the North Sea with their destination only a few hours away, Schroeder sat reading a book on the deck. A wiry man who's face appeared older than his movements, approached and asked if the chair next to Schroeder was unoccupied. His light jacket was open.

Schroeder nodded barely looking up and returned to his reading. He was feeling a bit safer, believing that if he was going to be approached it would have already happened, but he still kept a low profile. However, his mind raced as his thoughts kept encroaching on his ability to concentrate on the words in the book. He had reread several passages multiple times.

Just as he was beginning to think the visitor benign, two men in dark suits crowded his chair. He looked up. They stood impassive. One looked at him, the other turned away and scanned the deck. The man on the deck chair beside him spoke, "You didn't mention you were going to Russia, Mr. Schroeder."

"Who are you?"

"Why were you in Russia sir?"

"It is none of your business I'm afraid, but I was completing my research on the accoutrements of the nobility in the mid-1800's."

"I'll be blunt Herr Schroeder, we know what you have been doing. Your connections are all known to us. We need you to remember your German heritage and help us create a Greater Germany. We would like you to inform us about various aspects of British society and movements. We will have an agent contact you in England. Any indication that you have double crossed us and your life is forfeit and several members of your history department at the University of West London may not survive."

The two men turned and walked away, disappearing down a stair-case. The sitting man, rose, smiled a knowing smile, and left in the opposite direction. He was so completely without features in his manner, face, bearing and dress, that Schroeder realized he could not describe him should he be asked. There was simply nothing on which to hang a description. No scar, nor accent, nor mannerism that could be attached to him, yet he seemed the ringleader, and Schroeder expected he would be the man who surfaced once he arrived in England.

Schroeder cursed himself for getting involved in these matters. He stood by the rail as the ship began its final approach to Edinburgh harbour. A man he did not recognize stood beside him. As a young couple on the other side of him moved away down the deck the man said, "They have been watching you closely. I will take the key off ship and take it directly to Winston myself."

Schroeder looked confused and worried. The man pointed to the harbour like he was engaged in some geographic conversation.

"Oh, ah, preparation is the key."

Schroeder tried to clear his mind but the intentions of all these people swirled and he wondered if his mission had been compromised and they were all Russian agents. He exited the ship and moved to collect his luggage. He had arranged a hotel in Edinburgh for the night but seeing the train station across the street from his hotel he decided to make south, and caught a train that would get him to London late that night.

He got off the train in London, thinking himself wise for avoiding the hotel. But fearing the reach of the agents he had encountered he descended into the tube and headed for his west end home. He realized that heading home would not remove him from scrutiny but he could think of no other place he'd rather be, except maybe Pennsylvania.

Exiting the tube station, with few people about at the late hour, he was surrounded by two burly men and hustled into a car. Speed seemed to be their focus. HIs luggage was brutally whisked along, and tossed into the boot with as little ceremony as he had been. He sat in the back with one of the men, the other drove.

Schroeder was petrified. He sat, still without any movement to enhance his own comfort, still contorted from being pushed in, in the same position he had landed in, facing the opposite side of the car. He considered trying to leap from the vehicle but his back was to the door and he could not see the handle without giving away his intentions. The two men said nothing until they were away from the station.

"Jolly good, Professor, we'll make a spy out of you yet."

Schroeder remained alert. Who were these men?

"Oh, ah," the driver stumbled. "Preparation is the key," he said very slowly, enunciating every letter, in a Midlands accent, much different from the Scots lilt he had otherwise used. " Sorry , we aren't very good at this stuff. I'm gathering that we don't have a lot of cloak and dagger people, or the ones in practice are reserved for other missions."

"You've nearly given me a heart attack," Schroeder relaxed slightly. "Where are we going?"

"To a hotel south of the city tonight and a meeting with Winston tomorrow. Relax Professor, you were masterful to take that hotel room and then avoid it. Two Russians got off ship with you. They headed to the hotel. And the man you spoke to on deck this morning. Who was he?"

"German. They threatened me and my colleagues at the university."

"Not a good way to make friends, I think. We have dodged them all and the key is safely with us, and soon to be with Winston."

"What about the German agents?"

"We did put a tail on the gentleman who spoke to you."

"I thought you were watching."

"We were, and we saw it but didn't know who they were when

they approached you. It happened pretty quick and lasted all of 15 seconds. What did you see Gregory?"

"I saw a bit. I saw the first guy sit down and then the end of it as they all left. Strangely, I was asked to help an old lady carry some things up a couple of decks and could not refuse, thinking it would only be a minute. You know, up and down the stairs. Could I have been set up?"

"Like I said Professor, we are learning as we go."

"Won't they come looking for me once I go home?"

"The Russians, not likely. They will be watched and detained should any concerns arise. Remember, they have nothing on you save suspicion. And you have nothing incriminating. Now the Germans . . . ."

"They threatened me and people in my department."

"Oy, we'll have to do something about that, methinks."

"You are bloody well right. I am not a spy. I didn't ask for this."

"Sorry old chap, you are now. Or at least the Germans and the Russians think you are," he clipped a laugh. "Don't worry they won't do anything rash, they want you to help them. I bet the next visit from them will be all sugar and spice. And then we should know who they are. Who knows, perhaps Winston will set some-thing up with you to keep them dangling."

\* \* \* \* \* \* \* \* \*

The next morning Schroeder found himself at a small inn in Guildford. He was finishing breakfast when one of the escorts from the previous evening's car ride slid into a seat at his table.

"Come now Perfesser, we don't want to keep Winston waiting. Unhappy with his rough treatment but believing that a visit with Churchill would at least confirm that everything thrust at him was on the up and up, he drained his tea and followed the man to a waiting car.

Sure enough, they made their way to Chartwell by an expected route, through back roads, along single lane country tracks, avoiding towns, villages and people. More than once Schroeder wondered if he had fallen in with foreign agents. And even more remarkable was that England seemed empty of Englishmen. There were no people to be seen. Perhaps it was the early hour, he thought. Then out of nowhere the car was making the familiar approach to Chartwell and moments later he was escorted into the sitting room. Winston made his way in after a short time.

"I am so sorry for the brusque treatment, however my greeting committee saw the Russian agents and panicked a bit. As you, we are not terribly polished ourselves in this spy business. Very much out of practice."

Tommy here will spend a bit of time with you for the next few weeks. Oh, nothing to worry about. I've just asked him to keep an eye on you as the Russians and now apparently the Germans are likely to follow up. They are very suspicious of us and we of them."

"So why deal with them at all."

"Much to my dislike, at least with the Russians, we may end up birds of a feather before all this is over. We do not like each other but we both fear Hitler more. And frankly we would like to hear what they have to say to you."

Tommy here delivered the key last night. He got it from our man on board the ship, as we felt it was better to keep it an extra step away from those who were searching for you and your motives."

"You might have mentioned that to me."

"Best to limit information in things like this. Then nothing can slip or be coerced."

"I'd like to go home now, what should I tell the Russians when they show up?"

"Sell them the truth of your cover story. Believe it yourself. You were studying society weddings especially those of nobility from outside of Russia marrying into the country. Tommy will always be nearby should things get out of control, though I don't expect that to happen. I am fairly sure they have no definite knowledge of what you were doing."

"Except the fact that I stole the key."

"Well there is that. Good on you for getting it but you took an awful chance and now, if the Russians are meticulous with their artifacts, they know about our interests, though they cannot know why. As they knew your itinerary to some degree, I expect they will have agents running all over Europe looking for keys where ever you went."

Back in London, Professor Schroeder did not have to wait long for a knock at his door. On the evening of his return he was attended by two men of slight build, heavy coats and hats which appeared a bit oversized, giving them a menacing aspect, especially as the spring weather had turned warmer. They were almost comically dressed as spies with hats pulled low and beige trench coats to keep out the cooler night air.

"Ah Professor, we've met before. I am Alexi and this is Nicholai, you might remember us from the ship on your recent trip from Leningrad to Edinburgh."

The second man looked a bit familiar and Schroeder knew he had spoke with Alexi in Leningrad. "What can I do for you?"

"May we step in?"

"Ah, sorry, I am in the middle of an overdue project for the

University and have little time to spare."

"I will get to the point. One of us will call on you in the next few days, at a place of your choosing should you provide us with one, or of our choosing should you ignore our request."

"That does not seem friendly."

"It can be. All we want to know is will you act as a backdoor conduit for the Russian people and your English hosts. Given your recent travels, I assume of course that you have a contact in the British Foreign Office?"

Schroeder audibly sighed. "I see no harm in that. But I am hardly an international traveller, nor am I privy to anything of interest to anyone other than academics who study culture."

"But you have a plausible reason for travelling Europe, you evidently speak several languages and seem to have a link to the British government."

"I don't speak Russian."

"What about your aunt?"

"She speaks Russian but she married into our family and for her there was no one to speak it to."

"When can we meet with you?"

"I will be at the Rose and Thistle, a pub in Ealing on Wednesday at 4 p.m. But I may be there with a friend or two, tomorrow is a day where several acquaintances could drop by as it is well known that we frequent the pub that day of the week."

"Good evening, we will not keep you. One of us will attend the public house for a lengthier discussion. I am hopeful that you see your way clear to help us. We need a conduit. In the end Russia and England will have to act in concert."

"I do not want to do anything that will jeopardize my standing in this country, or at my University. I am not a spy, or a messenger, I have no contact in the Foreign Office, nor do I have any ties or loyalties to anyone other than myself."

"Come now Professor, your connections are obvious. I fully expect you will let your English contacts know of our approach. There is no harm in them knowing, that is the point of a go-between."

Schroeder stammered a denial but even he knew it was not convincing.

"And then, there is the matter of the key that you took."

Schroeder tried to form up a response and though it was a denial, it came out garbled and meaningless as his search for the right words failed him.

"It would be a shame if the British Foreign Office found out about your theft. It might blow up into an international incident."

Schroeder made his denial again, this time with a bit more confidence and closed the door. He sat down at his desk but could not concentrate even on the simplest organizational task.

He was eyes and ears in Britain for the United States, he was being recruited by the Russians as a messenger, though he feared going back to that country if they were aware of his light fingered approach to their artifact, and he was something of a low level agent for the shadow British government. And the Germans had leaned on him heavily.

# Chapter Five - Spring 1939

Schroeder returned to life in Ealing. He decided to extract himself from the merry-go-round of intrigue. He could not keep it all straight in his head and wanted no more complication.

Churchill had summoned him once again after the Russians had visited.

Standing with his brief case in a small meeting room at Westminster he burst out with it.

"I was approached by some Germans on the ship just before I landed, demanding I provide them with information or I and my colleagues would face violence. Then Russians appeared at my door two nights ago asking if I would be their messenger. Frankly I appear to be some sort of agent for everyone involved in this."

"It was Russians when you returned home?"

"They said they were Russians, had Russian names and accents, and they mentioned the key. One of them I recognized from Leningrad. And it was Germans on the ship. They referred to a

Greater Germany. The people that distracted Tommy."

"Don't you worry now, Professor Schroeder. I have a couple of men watching you."

"Tommy was apparently watching over me. It didn't work out. The Russians still made it to my door."

"You are still whole. And your mission for us is complete. All that we ask is that you don't let anyone else know about its true nature."

"But it seems as if everyone else knows more about it than I do."

"Write your piece. As I said I will help you get it published at some considerable profit to you. Start with a few teasing magazine pieces and promise a book. The publication of even one article should deflect some of the suspicion regarding your travels. A subsequent book on the subject will help as well. Though I understand that may take some time, time you do not believe you have. We will put another man on you as a body guard, should you like."

"I have Americans watching me, Germans, probably Russians who now want me to be a messenger for them, and have guaranteed another meeting whether I like it or not, and now you want another man to join the parade? There are so many people following me around there will be a trail of dust as they tramp about after me. That might be more suspicious than anything else I do. It seems everyone I speak to knows my business and has an angle on my loyalties."

"Here is my telephone number, direct. The other is my own body guard. If you are concerned call us. Otherwise you are free as previously described. However co-operation with our enemies is of course, a concern. Remember your oath. If you would like to volunteer information about what they are interested in, perhaps you can be of further use, a valuable tool should your loyalties come into question."

Schroeder took a deep breath.

"I simply want out of all of this, away from you, the Americans and especially my new found friends on the continent."

"Then be careful what you say and to whom. Deny, deny, deny, once you let slip a bit of information or an indication of cooperation they will renew their efforts to pull you in."

* * * * * * * * * *

Alexi was sitting in the pub when he entered. Schroeder almost turned on his heel when he saw him. His Russian look, with that slight oriental tilt to his features, made him easily recognizable despite having to leave his overcoat aside as spring deepened. With a second thought Schroeder figured that fleeing was pointless and that he had no real reason to avoid Alexi. He went directly to his table and sat down. He wanted to get the whole business sorted out and put behind him.

Alexi said nothing.

"I am not a spy. I do not like this stuff. I am a poor academic who studies things that may shed light on our fractured European culture."

"We don't want you to spy sir. Does someone else ask this of you?"

"I am eyes and ears, and you want me for a messenger? I am not opposed to Russians, but I will only be involved in public. Legitimate government to legitimate government. I will tell anyone who asks about you and your desire to have me deliver messages. I have no plans to travel outside of Great Britain. My travelling is done and I have a book to write. On those terms you could deliver messages yourself and do not need to involve me."

"I cannot do it as I cannot get close to the government. And it is not the official government we want access to. You have a connection to Churchill and he is the linchpin in British policy. Our first message to Churchill is this . . . . 'Stalin expects Hitler will soon sign a non-aggression pact with us. We have read Mein Kampf. We know it will not be honored and are party to it only to buy time. We request help in our defence of Mother Russia. Help will allow us to engage much of the German army's strength and take away the pressure of a possible invasion of England.' Please deliver this message as soon as you can and provide me with any reply when I next visit with you. If anyone asks, I am a former colleague at the University, now at the Sorbonne and on sabbatical doing some research in London."

"I could expose you."

"Then you would expose yourself. Contact with foreign agents is in itself damning. Admitting to contact with foreign agents after the passage of time will cast a shadow of doubt on you."

"I have already told them of our contact."

"Then I am exposed. And they have not interfered. Perhaps Churchill wants this back door conduit between countries with similar interests."

"And how do I know of your sincerity?"

"Contact your aunt. She has gratefully accepted our offer to restore family property to her. Feel free to tell her anything you would like. We have no secrets."

"I thought you wanted to go through me?"

"Your unwillingness to help required that we expedite matters."

With that, Alexi drained his glass, got up and prepared to leave. "I am coming to enjoy this British beer. But I really want some good Russian vodka." He smiled at the thought.

Schroeder was on his second pint when Anderson slid into a seat at his table.

"Who was that you were talking to?"

Schroeder was determined to tell it straight, as he knew he could never keep up with a plethora of lies, especially shades of the truth tailored for differing interests.

"It was a Russian agent I met on my research trip to Leningrad, he wants me to be a messenger between Russia and Britain. While making it seem all on the up and up, he has been remotely threatening. But there hasn't been any violence yet, and I refuse to be cloak and dagger about it. So now you know."

Anderson was quiet, the information surprised him.

"They contacted you on your trip?"

"Yes, and so did the Germans."

"Seems like everyone is interested in Christoph Schroeder. What is the message?"

"They will shortly sign an non-aggression pact with Hitler but believe Hitler will soon violate the agreement. They want British assistance."

Anderson took the information without verbal comment, however his eyes and body language gave away his shock at the apparent cooperation between the bitter enemies.

"So you will deliver the message to Churchill? What exactly where you doing in Russia?"

"I was researching the wedding customs of the nobility, especially that of the British who married into noble families in Russia. Churchill has connections in publishing. My department dean put me on to him. Remember, I'm an academic. Publish or perish."

"That happened?"

"Yes, in fact the mother of Czarina Alexandria was a daughter of Queen Victoria."

"Oh that, I knew that, or close enough to it. So what can you tell me about Russia?"

"They are deeply suspicious of everyone and do not trust Hitler. I was only in Leningrad, so I could not ascertain any construction projects or any munitions build up. I had a minder at all times. There is a fatalism in the streets and among the populace. They know the future will be one of sacrifice."

"Any more contact with Churchill?"

"Only when I returned from a similar trip to Spain. When I was there the Spanish government took the opportunity to ask me on behalf of the British to take several crates of Spanish museum artifacts for safe keeping during their conflict. I agreed. Churchill wanted to get a sense of the government's mood regarding their civil war."

"And you told him?"

"Yes, I thought the fact they had given me crates of items, spoke volumes."

"No, what did you tell him?"

"Exactly that. I have little understanding of the background of that civil war, nor any real sense of any posturing. Having me read into anything that happened there would be a huge mistake. I am not a spy."

"So you keep saying. But it appears that everyone in Europe disagrees with you."

* * * * * * * * *

Schroeder's second article on the weddings of the nobility was published in the Spectator in August. In addition to a substantial cheque, he received some feedback from the publishers who enjoyed the subject and his editorial stance of mild amusement at the doings of the titled subjects. A large publishing house contacted him about a substantial book on the subject, but the editor he spoke to seemed to have no enthusiasm for the subject, taking his involvement as a duty. He agreed to forward whatever he had completed at the end of summer. At that point they would make any alterations in tone and try to work out a publishing schedule.

The Russians and Germans signed their agreement in August. Schroeder forwarded a few chapters on non-specific marriages and the general customs of the 19th century. Specifics on British marriages would form the basis of future chapters.

The Germans invaded Poland in September dividing up the country with their new Russian friends. Schroeder took some time away from his home to write, returning to London just before the invasion of Poland. Prime Minister Chamberlain was unable to avoid his promises of coming to the aid of the Poles and war had been declared. Sentiments in England wavered. A deep seated fear of the Germans generated in the Great War, and the threats of Hitler seen against the duplicity of his actions, put the British squarely in opposition to Hitler, though largely unwillingly. The Chamberlain government wavered, but held fast, and dutifully declared war after trying unsuccessfully to find a way to avoid their promise to the Poles. The French followed suit, but both nations did little else, save a short French foray into German territory and a quick retreat back to the Maginot Line.

Churchill believed that the stunted French reaction was worse than simply doing nothing. Preparations were necessary but the huge French army had poked its head out of its hole to stare down the Germans and had disappeared without a trace, unwilling to engage. A French invasion at that moment might have changed the course of the war as the Germans had only a token force left on the French frontier. Hitler had gambled and won again. He seemed to know the French mind better than the French themselves.

Churchill sat at his dining room table, lunch successfully put away and several of the members of his intelligence group awaiting his word.

"It appears that Neville is sympathetic to the Germans. He is so blinded by his desire to remain at peace that he is actually considering some sort of treaty or pact with them.

"That will not turn out well for Britain," said one of the operatives at the table. "And it's a repudiation of centuries of British foreign policy."

"You are bloody right it will not turn out well for us," thundered Churchill. The man was at the same time cowed by the power of Churchill's voice and thrilled he had been recognized as having quickly grasped the situation.

"Our saving grace is that the majority of parliament agrees with us. Neville cannot long hang on."

"And you will be asked to assume the office?"

"Not for certain, I'm afraid. There are a few others he will consider and he doesn't like me; thinks I'm a warmonger and all that rot and nonsense. Choosing me suggests he was wrong all along."

"He was."

"Politicians have a strong desire to avoid admitting that fact. Bureaucrats too. I speak from experience."

With the declaration of war, Chamberlain formed a war cabinet. In an effort to gain co-operation from his opponents he included his own Party nemesis Churchill, who became First Lord of the Admiralty, and representatives of the Labor Party and the Social

Democrats, among his own inner circle of supporters. Churchill's constant crowing about the German threat and his track record of being right about their actions had all but insured he would be included.

As the First Lord, Churchill had several meetings in London, most of which were conducted in his new flat at the Admiralty Office, a very convenient location, south of Trafalgar Square. Having been First Lord of the Admiralty previously, it amused him to see much of what he had wrought still in place and he was pleased with the genuine happiness that his return to the office seemed to bring to many of the long time Admiralty staff.

Despite the challenges of his first appointment before and in the early stages of the previous war, the staff knew he could be counted on as a strong supporter of the British Navy, its traditions and importance to the nation's defence.

Fresh from his consultation with his own shadow Foreign Office, he maintained the difficult position of showing loyalty to Chamberlain while opposing his every move and jockeying to position himself as the obvious choice to replace the Prime Minister should his government become untenable. It was a balancing act that had to hold until the inevitable came to pass.

However Churchill's most important meeting was at Buckingham Palace. He had been summoned by King George VI.

"Winston, how good of you to come."

The formality of that statement always rang hollow with Churchill, who was a monarchist but knew he had been summoned. To avoid the meeting carried an historic significance that was at least Cavalier, so much so that he personally and historically was beholden to the call.

"Your Majesty, I am always at your service and the service of your House."

"Yes, thank you for that, but the Queen is s-still unhappy with you on that front. Your s-support for Mrs. S-Simpson is s-still bitter to her. My brother however adores you. And it is on that, that I wanted to s-speak to you. We are now at war, even if no s-shots have yet been fired."

Churchill nodded, listening.

"My brother, the former King, who you admire so deeply, has been approached by representatives of the German government acting on instructions from Herr Hitler himself. They are proposing a truce and a s-summit regarding possible co-operation between Germany and Britain."

Churchill spluttered but no coherent words came out.

"Edward assures me these people are the future. All they s-seek is a unification of all Germanic peoples  and the s-space in which their nation can flourish."

"At whose expense?"

"Edward tells me our support will assure the s-stability of the Continent, long acknowledged as the basis of our foreign policy."

"Your Majesty, aligning with the Nazis will give them license to run roughshod over Europe and become the dominant power there. There will be no stability without German ambitions held in check. It is our national policy to oppose anyone becoming too strong in Europe, to maintain the balances of power."

"My brother is quite persuasive, and quite s-sure of himself."

"But you are King."

"And you dear Winston might s-soon be Prime Minister. Neville knows he cannot long hang on. I have had a discussion with him on this matter and he will entertain a delegation to at least hear what they have to s-say. If there is a chance to avoid a general conflict, given the bloodletting of the Great War, it s-seems reasonable to explore it. If he is able to delay the conference it will give us s-some time to become more prepared, s-should nothing come of the talks. You are here as I thought you s-should know given the position you are in, your s-strong belief regarding Herr Hitler, and the possibility that Edward is wrong."

"Well, at least there is that. Thank you Your Majesty. Perhaps I should speak with Edward. Is he in Paris?"

"Yes, for now but plans are afoot for moving him out of harm's way should it become necessary. I have given my blessing to this conference in hopes we can avoid war."

"I'm afraid the cost of avoiding war now will be too high."

"Time will tell on that."

"Unfortunately the Czechs and the Poles would disagree."

King George took a long look at Churchill. "You will make a formidable Prime Minister, Winston. I am s-stuck in a difficult place, as you might imagine. And wedged as I am, with limited powers of persuasion over people who are quite s-sure of them-selves."

And with that Churchill took his leave of the King and Buckingham Palace and was whisked by car at his instruction to Windsor Castle. He entered by a side entrance, a few of the staff wide-eyed at his unexpected arrival.

He summoned a trusted attendant and requested a meeting urgently.

Churchill was escorted along a number of hallways and then upstairs into the family living quarters. He had never been in this part of the castle. Waiting in a drawing room for a few minutes the door opened and the teenaged Princess Elizabeth entered. The door shut behind her.

"Sir Winston, I am so glad you could come," she said.

"Frankly Princess, I was unaware that you summoned me. I have just been in conference with your father and decided we needed to speak."

"That is why I summoned you. Your instincts on this matter are precise." The Princess sat down and motioned Churchill to a nearby chair.

"My mother is most concerned. My father is drifting into the orbit of his older, but not wiser brother. Plainly put, Edward is a Nazi, beyond even being a sympathizer, he subscribes to the ordering of society suggested by Herr Hitler. And worse, he wants it for Britain. I'm not sure what my father told you, he probably sugar-coated it, but Hitler is seeking an alliance with us, with an eye on a Saxon marriage with him as Prime Minister and my father as King."

Churchill stood stunned but unmoved. He scarcely blinked as he took in the implications.

"Determined to avoid war, Neville is sympathetic. My father too, primarily because of his brother's influence. My mother has repeatedly reminded my father of his brother's history of poor judgement."

"I have to think on this for a time. Off the top, it appears as if I must engineer Neville's resignation as PM. A daunting task if I am to keep future expectations in place. I have to consider every-thing, the implications are staggering. I do have some good news, we have retrieved the final key from the Russians."

"I think we need to open the box as quickly as possible, if only to know what it contains. I have not told my father about our efforts to get the keys. He has not mentioned the legend to me lately but I have seen him eyeing the desk as he walks by. He is thinking about it."

"We must remain a step ahead. If he asks after the keys I will not be able to lie to him."

* * * * * * * * * *

Churchill and the Princess arranged to meet at the Castle a few days later as both the King and Queen were at Buckingham Palace.

Churchill strode beside the Princess, though he took care to remain a hair behind her as she walked through Windsor Castle to the Long Gallery of St. George's Hall. Still a teen, the Princess had demonstrated a keen understanding of Britain and the world. Churchill was a bit skeptical due to her age but could not fault her choices and determination. As she had hinted, he suspected the work of her mother behind her effort.

Halfway along the great gallery lies a doorway to the Grand Reception Room and just outside this large double door was a writing table, its top displaying a beautiful and intricate wooden inlaid map of Europe. It showed the principle cities, rivers and mountains but curiously did not feature any political boundaries. It had been made at Queen Victoria's request soon after she became Queen Regnant.

"This is it. Now give me the keys."

He reverently handed her the first key.

"This is Russia. It cost at least one man his life."

"Enough with the cheap dramatics Sir Winston. One life may be a tragedy but it is nothing compared to the coming conflagration of Europe."

She brushed her hand over the map and a flap of wafer thin inlaid wood slid open and a keyhole was exposed in the area of Russia. She plunged the key deeply into the slot and twisted it with a click.

"That seems to have taken. Next."

Churchill handed her another key, telling her it was German. This was the key made from a mould and did not feature the semi-precious stones of the others. She performed the same ritual but this time without the click.

They managed to insert the keys from Spain and Denmark both of which clicked, appearing to have completed their purpose.

Then the Princess produced a key with an elaborate head, with precious stones inlaid in a Victorian emblem of the Empire. She softly inserted the key and turned it with a click.

In unison and almost comically they both looked up and around down the long length of the hall in both directions. Churchill notices and could not suppress a grin. The Princess noticed and giggled, but she remained fixed on her task. Assured they were alone, Churchill nodded to the Princess to open the lid.

The Princess reached under what appeared to be a table top and lifted gently. It did not move. She tried another method this time from below the entire box of the table. Nothing. She slid her hands along the sides of the smoothly stained wooden box which formed the desk top, hoping to find some loose panel or indication of an opening. She found it along the left and right sides. Playing with them she eventually poked them at both ends and at the point where the inlaid panel was at the back of the map box. The inch wide wooden panel poked in, swinging with a click on pegs built into the wood above and below the panel.

"Handles I think."

Grasping the two pieces of wood at each side of the desk she lifted. Then she pulled, and pushed and back and forth up and down. Nothing. She tried again to find more loose panels and manipulated the two she had found, pulling on them and pushing them in.

Nothing.

"I can only conclude Sir Winston that one or more of the keys is not right. And given the lack of a click from the German key, and the fact that it is a reproduction from a plaster cast, it must be flawed in some way."

Churchill was perplexed. He reached in and reinserted the German key, again without a click. He tried the others in turn, they all turned with a satisfactory click. He compared the German key to the others, looking for a common bit that might be missing from the German key.

"It appears you are right, I shall take it back and try to have it recast after anticipating what it's flaw might be."

"And I ask you to take the keys your brought with you and I will return the Victoria key to its place lest its absence be noticed."

"And when will you tell your father about this?"

"I'm not sure. I believe I will know when the time is right by future events."

"With the people in fear of German bombs, I cannot think it should be much longer, at least once we manage to open the box. According to your father a peace conference with the Germans is being organized. Chamberlain will soon inform cabinet but I expect he will not characterize the agenda. They will come to England which I see as a significant sign that they are serious and determined to have us on their side."

"You know that cannot happen. No matter what my father or Chamberlain say."

"I know it, and I think most of parliament know it, but I fear the possibility of an illusion of peace within easy reach might sway their resolve. Chamberlain has his allies. He did not become Prime Minister without some ability to persuade."

"While we are here, try to lift the table." She looked up and down the long hallway. There was no one, not even the usual attendant at either end.

Churchill took his position and reached under the boxy table top with both arms and lifted.

"Is it bolted to the floor?" He looked at the legs for indications of fastenings.

The Princess shook her head. He tried again, this time much more determined. It rose a mite off the floor on the two legs at the back of the table, those at the front, perhaps cleared the hardwood floor but it was difficult to tell. Tiny half moons of dust traced near the front legs, indicating it had been moved.

She told him to replace it but he could not. In the end the Princess ducked down and cleaned the dusty evidence away with her finger.

"Let me know when you are ready for a second try."

Churchill bowed low and strode down the hall. He knew the way out.

* * * * * * * * *

Churchill returned a few days later and he and the Princess made their way to St. George's Hall, this time entering through the Grand Reception Hall which opened up on St. George's Hall right beside the small writing table.

"Quickly, attendants have been called away for a meeting. We only have a few minutes."

They repeated the key procedure the same as before, this time the German key made a satisfying click as it was turned. They both looked at each other with raised eye brows.

"I hate to admit it, but the impression we had of the German key did not have the point at its business end, that meant we were pushing the key in a bit too deeply. All the others had a uniform point. Easy to see once I looked for it."

The Princess flipped out the handles from the lower side of the table box and she lifted. Nothing. She grabbed the handles, turned them so the narrowest side was perpendicular to the ground and she forcefully pulled them forward. They slid toward the front of the box. She lifted them. Nothing. Then she turned them back to their original alignment with the narrow parts facing the ceiling and the floor. They clicked. With a look of triumph she lifted them. The map top smoothly lifted up, held by hinges cut into the wooden top at the far edge of the table. The metal nature of the box was immediately evident, as the majority of the space was taken up by thick metal and the locking mechanisms. In fact the box, which looked to be about 18 inches deep from the outside was really only three inches deep, the rest was a thick metal plate and the ornate Victorian locks.

However that was not what the Princess nor Churchill saw at first. Inside the shallow box enclosure was a band of silvery metal formed into a circlet that was forged but imperfect. It was less than an inch in height and perhaps a quarter inch wide. At what appeared to be the front, the metal curved up and was thicker, forming a setting for a large ruby, perhaps an inch in diameter. This ruby was surrounded by smaller white stones, likely diamonds, of perhaps a bit less than a carat each. They were cut but not as precisely as one would expect. It was not a modern piece.

The circlet sat on a piece of parchment with a few ornately written words visible inside the circle of metal.

"What is it?"

"It's a crown of some sort, and it looks very old. The stones are cut with skill but without modern tools. I am not sure, but it looks like something I've seen before."

"Really?"

"A drawing in a book. My memory is very clear, I believe this is the ancient crown of the Holy Roman Emperor, made for Charles the Great, Charlemagne, when he assumed his title in 800 AD. We will have to subtlety confirm this though."

"How does one confirm such a thing? Charlemagne is unavailable."

"I need to find the book. I'd like to credit my background, schooling and deep understanding of European history but I admit it matches a drawing I saw in a schoolbook I used when I was a boy at Blenheim. It had been my father's and grandfather's, the 7th Duke. It likely preceded him. The family was prodigious in cataloguing things, but they likely did not stoop to children's school books," he laughed. "We shall see."

The Princess smiled, Winston was charming, funny and had the ability to take charge of his background without making it obvious. She did not need to.

"I understood from my man in the field that Hitler acquired or confiscated the Austrian crown jewels immediately after they annexed Austria. Those crown jewels have long been associated with the later stages of the institution of Holy Roman Empire. I imagine this crown either went missing, seeing as we have it, or it was lost to history as the modern Holy Roman crown came into use. What we have here might be something quite different. As you know there are ceremonial crowns, usually very ornate. And then there are crowns that are used in everyday circumstances. This must be the latter type. What we need is an expert who can corroborate my memories or dash them."

"Can you find one and be subtle about it?"

"I'm going to have to. But first, look for an inscription on the circlet. It may shed some light."

The Princess lifted the crown. "The metal is quite heavy."

Can you see anything on it, inside and out?"

She carefully inspected it. "Yes, there are words in script. Latin saying, 'P Me Reges Regnant' or 'By Me Kings Reign'."

"But what of the parchment? Take it out and read it."

Elizabeth reached in and took the parchment replacing the circlet in its place.

The document was folded and contained several sheets. She opened it. "It's written in Latin."

"I assume you can read it. What does it say?"

"It appears to be a treaty," Elizabeth gasped. "It is written in very formal Latin. It's between King George III and Frederick William II of Brandenburg, King of Prussia, and dated 17 August, 1785."

Elizabeth's eyes scanned the document. She began to translate.

"In memory of our close co-operation in the War of Spanish Succession, English efforts in the Low Countries to defeat the Bourbon usurpers and to secure the rights and privileges of the Hapsburg Holy Roman Empire, King Frederick II has already bestowed honours upon selected Englishmen. And now with the efforts of Frederick II to help the British with the services of Hessian troops to fight against the rebels in America, King George III pledges to honour this treaty between Germanic and British peoples, who have emerged from the same historic stock, to remain allied in advancement of our peoples, to help each other succeed and to officially join our efforts together only in the direst need."

"Oh my God," said Churchill. "My own ancestor is mixed up in this. The First Duke was a knight of the Holy Roman Empire. We thought the honour was ceremonial."

"There is more, it seems to outline our ties, lay out some territorial

84

limitations, and a desire to keep this understanding a secret as much as possible. They wanted to avoid others joining together to oppose them."

Churchill stood pondering. "Well that certainly explains some odd-ments of British history: why the Germans never challenged Britain in India, why both parties seemed strangely apart and uninterested in each other in Africa, and how they kept the French, particularly Napoleon at bay, and the British disinterest in the Franco-Prussian war of 1871. Perhaps there is a reason this did not apply during the Great War?"

"Maybe it was forgotten in the late Victorian period?"

"How could that be when this arrangement of artifacts appears to be placed by Victoria herself?"

"As you can already see, Sir Winston, there is much in heaven and earth for which we have not yet discovered an explanation."

He lifted his head and gazed at the Princess with a keen eye.

"You, my dear Princess, are wise beyond your years. You frighten me not a little."

Princess Elizabeth's expression did not change but she felt a flush of pride at the compliment.

* * * * * * * * * *

A few weeks later Churchill sent a note to Princess Elizabeth.

"Three cheers on my memory. Apparently I was right. The circlet was apparently incorporated into the Austrian's more modern version of the crown but had gone missing sometime in the 18th century. In this way the Hapsburgs could give it away without apparently losing anything. It was bestowed in advance of the formal treaty to bind William and Mary to the Hapsburgs. I have also confirmed that my ancestor, the First Duke, was a titled Prince of the Holy Roman Empire. That honour was bestowed upon him and others at the time of Frederick Wilhelm II."

Churchill turned the information over in his mind. He did not doubt that Hitler knew of the crown and wanted it, likely as a token of their past cooperation and future agreements. The crown itself would be a great bargaining chip he thought. He was determined not to let the current King George or Chamberlain know of its discovery, at least for now.

And if Hitler wanted George VI to be the king of the new Saxon Kingdom, a new Prussian state, then the crown would go to him by right. Hitler's determination to get the crown might be a signal as to how serious he was about the combination of kingdoms. It struck Churchill that if George VI would be offered the crown, whoever eventually married the Princess would become the heir and eventually king of a combined realm. He shuddered at the thought that Hitler had already considered all of this and probably had a suitable match, advantageous to the Germans, already selected.

# Chapter Six - November 1939

Three German envoys, all sharply dressed and accompanied by three military men clad in black dress uniforms landed at a small aerodrome west of London. One of the military men was an interpreter, though all the men appeared to speak impeccable English. Two said they were educated in Britain as the sons of men in the German foreign service.

Few members of the British government had been informed of the visit. Churchill, despite being First Lord of the Admiralty and in the war cabinet, was not one of them. Chamberlain had taken the unprecedented step of whisking the envoys from the air landing strip to nearby Beaumont College, a former country house located a few miles west of the aerodrome, minimizing any contact with locals, stray members of the press and even curious members of the government.

The irony of the Prime Minister himself being secretive about his intentions did not escape Chamberlain who nevertheless assented to the arrangement.

Only the headmaster of the College knew of the meeting, and without being privy to any details had been sworn to strict secrecy by Chamberlain himself. He arranged for the parties to be escorted into a secondary entrance, and taken to a little used sitting room of the ancient estate in a wing that was essentially mothballed by the small college.

As a college, it was not unusual for day visitors or conference attendees to arrive at the front entrance, but four limousines would have stirred local eyes to consider that something unusual was afoot. It was beneficial that the extensive grounds allowed for several entrances and means of travel.

One of the German military men remained with the vehicles. He was openly carrying a sidearm. A fact the British, including Chamberlain, noted.

"Please sir, this is a school. I ask you please to put that weapon aside or at least under your coat." It appeared that the Germans in the meeting were sensitive enough to not attempt to enter the building armed.

The rooms had been spruced up for the visit, but only a rudimentary cleaning and a small tea service were in evidence. Chamberlain had two suited aides providing security for the room, standing out in the hall, to ensure no one blundered into the meeting. Another remained with the cars and their German minder, to deflect anyone away from the site. This despite the fact that the cars had been removed from casual view as much as possible, parking them around a corner of the building.

"I'm sorry for our lack of hospitality but I think you understand how sensitive these discussions are, especially considering we are currently in a declared state of war."

"Yes, Mr. Chamberlain, it is quite alright. But we felt the need to speak face to face, to get a true picture of where our countries stand."

The group was now seated around a large dining room table on the upper floor of an older wing of the house, once the De Vere - Beaumont House and now a college, owned by the county and used sparingly for meetings and events on its sprawling grounds.

After serving a round of tea and having a few plates of sandwiches placed before them, Chamberlain opened the discussion.

"Frankly gentlemen, your offer has been received here with some skepticism, many Members of our House of Commons do not trust German promises after the string of . . . reversals . . . in recent years."

"Mr. Prime Minister it is unfortunate that our actions appear as such, but we gave various assurances and indications regarding our actions, based on circumstances at the time. If those circum-stances were changed, if forces outside of our control take actions we do not expect, then we have to change our guidance. Events outside of our control or anticipation can alter things rapidly. As you know violence initiated by minority interests was rapidly escalating in the areas where most Germans wanted a union. We had to take steps to prevent bloodshed by extremists."

"Or you were preventing opposition from becoming organized. But we are not here to bicker. And that being said gentlemen, we here in Britain want to see substantial proof that any agreement we make will be upheld and honoured. Herr Hitler has used minor changes in situations to make major changes to his proffered policies. It is very disconcerting to us."

Chamberlain looked around the room, focussing on each of the German negotiators in turn, using his powers of persuasion as well as he knew how.

He continued, "Entering into an agreement, the scope of which you propose, is impossible without a track record of faith and trust between the two parties. We have been faithful to our bargains. Herr Hitler has stretched the credibility of our belief in his honesty."

The lead German envoy shifted in his seat, preparing his remarks.

"We of course take issue with that statement, however your perception is now the reality and so we propose to take no aggressive action on your Declaration of War. We will not fight back nor advance anymore, while you consider our proposals."

"And what about the French?"

"The French are different from the rest of us, they are not Saxons, nor Teutonic in nature. Herr Hitler has nothing against the French but he is not inclined to side with them as they have proved to be unreliable given their unlikely view of the world. I'm sure you have seen it yourself, the French are not committed, they have no view of the future and see themselves and their civilization as superior to all others, despite evidence to the contrary. Here I will cite their myopic world view and the decadent nightclub scene of Paris as evidence. In addition, the French declined to immediately invade Germany after our Polish police action, despite their assurances to the Poles. Perhaps that was for the best as we believe war can be avoided. It is another act of faithlessness from a nation whose word counts for nothing."

"Are there any other assurances you can provide?"

"War has been declared. How much time, without aggressive actions will constitute enough for you to believe our sincerity? Mr. Prime Minister I would like to invite you to Berlin, but given the parliamentary declaration you have made that would appear to be impossible. You will have to determine the depth of our good will yourselves. Upon seeing our lack of aggression to your declaration, the first course of action would be to withdraw that Declaration of War through a public peace initiative. Remember you have agreed to step in against us with several of our Greater German partners and you have failed to hold yourself to your own high standards. Presumably as conditions changed which produced those declarations, you altered your world view. We are equally concerned about your trustworthiness. The British determination to side with the loathsome French in the Great War came as a shock given our longstanding treaty."

"Treaty? What treaty? Certainly you are not citing the Austrian Accords of 1795? We considered your actions in the Great War a repudiation of that."

"Now Mr. Prime Minister, we had a treaty of co-operation in full force and you, who had for centuries been opposed to the French, came in on their side in 1914. So who repudiated the treaty? We can argue the causes of the previous conflict or we can acknowledge the state of historic co-operation between our peoples. And we too are uncertain about current British motives. Certainly the provisional government in Czechoslovakia wonders after your sincerity. The Poles have that belief, given that you've only postured and declared but done nothing concrete."

Chamberlain was thoughtful. The German envoy was persuasive.

"What about your agreement with Stalin?"

"We have made an agreement with the Soviets, but we fear it will not hold, that they are merely buying time to invade us, as our anti-communist beliefs stand in the way of their communist deter-mination to dominate the world. In the end Mr. Prime Minister, a strong Germany is the best bulwark against the Red Menace. It will come down to a fight against the communists and we hope you are with us in that fight. This is partly why we would speak now, before anyone becomes too entrenched in their actions, similar to the machinations of nations prior to the Great War. Our Treaty with the Austrians and your treaty with the French put us both in difficult circumstances in light of our treaty with each other. Once the Great War began each side became entrenched in their positions and could not reverse course. Had we spoken before it occurred, perhaps much of it could have been avoided. I remind you of the British position during the Franco-Prussian War of 1870 -1."

Even Chamberlain was uncomfortable with the threat of a communist push backed by Russia. Chamberlain felt the German's words, and each was a body blow to British policy. Accusations that the British were untrustworthy stung. There was a ring of truth to such concerns.

"Perhaps we should speak again in the coming months, once we have seen your determination to remain unconcerned with our current war footing."

"A wise idea Prime Minister," the German smiled, stretching out his hand. "We too are looking for assurances, and your faith in this pause in hostilities will give us some belief that you are sincere in renewing our long standing ties. I understand through Edward Windsor, that his brother, your King, is sympathetic to a formal dual kingdom and intrigued by the idea or renewed co-operation."

"He has not dismissed it out of hand, however our ancient parliament will have to survive in some form - perhaps a dual parliamentary system in the early days of any agreement, for this to pass scrutiny of our ruling classes. If we are to proceed it must be with small, deliberate steps."

"Agreed. The disposition of parliaments is an idea for a more fully rounded discussion. We have bandied about the idea of separate representative bodies with a third joint house dealing strictly with international issues. In addition, Herr Hitler has asked me to inquire after a trifle that Edward Windsor mentioned in passing, that the British Royal Family holds. It is a piece of the Austrian crown jewels that was sent to England many years ago, apparently to solidify the understanding of co-operation between Frederick the Great of Prussia and your King George III. Herr Hitler would like to reunite it with the Austrian set from which it has been missing. Your willingness to return the piece would be a significant sign of your good will in this matter."

Chamberlain's eyes widened. "Oh, well I know of no such thing, but I can certainly look into it. You say Edward is aware of it. Perhaps his brother, the King, knows something too."

"It is Herr Hitler's wish, with your agreement, that this circlet be used to crown George VI as King of our union. If you agree to participate we can work out the logistics of parliaments, the duties of the King and Chancellor. It is believed that a loose association be enacted with more powers and obligations coming as both parties become more comfortable with the arrangement."

Both sides bandied about requirements that would arise should such an alliance be created. The Germans were pleased that the discussions reached that point as it indicated that the British had not dismissed the notion out of hand.

Eventually the German rose from his chair and bowed slightly.

"We will kindly be leaving for home. We will let our government know your concerns and will seek a time for a second conference, perhaps around Christmastime. I hope that you or your representatives can come to visit us. Germany is lovely at that time of year."

The Germans were escorted by the Prime Minister back to their waiting plane and they left.

"I'm not sure what to think about all that," said Chamberlain as the German plane receded into the distance. "It doesn't hurt to talk, and buying a little time will make Winston happy as he has more time to prepare. Though he will howl when he hears about this proposal, and he will howl louder when he understands the

King is interested."

"It's a pity we didn't prosecute the old man for treason or something when we found out about his parallel foreign office activities."

"We've been through all of that. It kept him busy, and frankly it was good to get information that was not first vetted by the pro-German group in our official Foreign Office. When the two bits of information agreed we knew we at least had a modicum of truth."

"Well Winston is going to have to be brought up to speed on this now that he is First Lord of the Admiralty and in the war cabinet."

"In the meantime let me think on it, we have a cabinet meeting tomorrow. And I need to have a talk with the King."

# Chapter Seven

"Well Mr. Chamberlain I do kn-know about the 'trifle' that Herr Hitler s-seeks. A family s-s-story, you know. I think I kn-know where it is, but I have n-never s-seen it. It is quite s-s-securely locked away."

King George then told Chamberlain about the desk, its weight and the lack of keys to open it. He declined Chamberlain's offer to try to force it open, reminding the Prime Minister that the desk seemed to be made of wood, but it was very, very heavy, and obviously a safe of some kind.

"We could simply cut through the metal. The desk might be destroyed but in the face of a broad European war that seems a small price to pay."

Chamberlain had the King show him the desk. The King had the Victoria key and put it in its place but without the other keys he was unable to open it. Chamberlain managed to find the movable side panels that functioned as a final lock and handles for the lid but without the keys they were simply curiosities. The weight of the desk confirmed the King's suspicions, that is was a safe disguised as a desk to hide in plain sight.

Princess Elizabeth had been watching activity in St. George's Hall, regularly taking detours in her travels around the castle to walk past the desk.

One day she saw tell-tale dusty half moons around the feet of the desk. It had been moved. She seripticiously brushed the dust away with her finger and guiltily looked around to make sure she was not observed.

She summoned Winston seeking his advice.

"You must remove the items and hide them. If your father is looking for the contents, they should be right out of the Castle. I expect they will try to cut the desk open, and very soon. There is a cabinet meeting tomorrow and  perhaps I will find out more, but my contacts in the Foreign Office say there has been a secret meeting with German envoys, somewhere in Hampshire. We had been told they wanted a meeting but that it has already occurred is a revelation."

"I will let you know if my father starts inquiring about keys. But what if he manages to open it and finds nothing?"

"Then he finds nothing and might drop the matter, or dismiss the myth as just that. He doesn't know for certain what is in there. The only way he can get in is to destroy it. And upon finding nothing, he is unlikely to ask you if you opened the box as it appears impervious to anything but the necessary keys or great violence. And what are the chances that an innocent Princess would possess the keys. You must make an effort to leave no trace that the circlet was in that box, once you've removed it. If you give it and the parchment to me, you can truthfully say you do not have it if questioned. I expect that no one would even think of you as the prime mover in this. But pray, let's hope it doesn't come to that.

For my part I will investigate these rumors of meetings with the Nazis."

The Princess looked pensive, "Sir Winston, I have kept my mother apprised of our plans."

Churchill straightened up to his full height, took a deep breath of air. "Do we have to worry about her?"

"I think not. She is violently opposed to Edward and might be the only person able to keep her secrets from the King without reprisals."

"So your counsel has been her counsel?"

"Yes, it was she who put me up to this task."

"In that case we should proceed as planned. Let's get the items away from anyone who might use them improperly. Don't tell your mother that we have removed the contents except in the most dire circumstance. That way she can easily say she did not open the box nor disperse the contents."

* * * * * * * * *

The next morning dawned a deep autumn day in London, with the first hint of winter to come. Churchill left the Admiralty and walked down Whitehall to Downing Street, tipped his hat to the guard at the front door of Number 10 and was admitted and directed to the cabinet room upstairs.

He was first to arrive, though soon the other members of the war cabinet drifted in with Chamberlain himself striding through the doors with only a minute to spare. He looked about the chamber and nodded finding his place and tapping a small gavel on a block to begin the meeting.

Two secretaries sat along the wall to record the proceedings. Each of the Ministers had an assistant there and they were all sitting along the wall at the far end of the room.

Chamberlain asked after each Minister's war preparedness and appeared satisfied with the answers. Churchill made his report, quite conscious to appear in simpatico with the Prime Minister but unable to hide the fact that Britain was woefully behind on war production, especially airplanes, to counteract an expected bombardment from the Germans.

"I have tasked Lord Beaverbrook with increasing our aircraft manufacturing. There are already signs of his success."

"Beaverbrook? Newspapermen know how to build planes?"

"Beaverbrook is an industrialist. He cuts through the bureaucracy and achieves his goals without pandering to anything that might hinder his success. We must remain mindful that actions are necessary, hard tangible production lay at the end of that approach."

"The Admiralty is interested in airplanes?" questioned a cabinet member.

"The Admiralty uses planes to defend the seas and our ships along our coasts and in port. Of course, Beaverbrook will be in touch with our munitions offices, as his production will be available to the Army Air Wing."

That explanation appeared to calm any further issue of Churchill acting beyond his responsibilities.

"And so we wait," said Chamberlain. "Delays in actually fighting this war are to our advantage. We have been able to delay any significant action for two reasons. First, Herr Hitler is busy shoring up his occupation of Poland. The Poles have fought bravely but it is hopeless as they are outmanned, outgunned and in a pincer on three sides. Large numbers of Polish nationals are sympathetic to the Germans. We do not have the ability to jump into the breach and Hitler knows it. And in any event his Navy is patrolling the Baltic in case we should try to intervene directly."

"The French made a push, I understand."

"Small and insignificant. For show actually. I imagine they hoped Hitler would back down immediately and when he did not the French fled. They refused to commit their troops and only made a show of fulfilling their treaty obligations before pulling back to the safety of the Maginot Line. In some ways their restraint has kept a lid on the powder keg. In other ways their lack of action may have emboldened Hitler."

"The Nazis will not respect the Line, they will go around it through Belgium. And being mechanized they will move quickly if they are not stopped."

"The First Lord of the Admiralty apparently knows the ins and outs of land battle strategy. Aren't we lucky to have such a man with us. I'm told with certainty from our Foreign Office that with their mechanized troops, the Germans are limited to existing paved roads, all of which lead to substantial defensive fortifications," said Chamberlain.

"They will come through the Ardennes," said Churchill.

"Really, a huge land force will flit through the forest on narrow, muddy tracks to attack an entire nation? And they will do it without significant roads or infrastructure?"

"They did it in the last war."

"On horseback, and we stopped them. Now they are limited by their mechanization strategy. But that leads me to reason number two for the quiet on the front." Chamberlain shuffled some papers. He cleared his throat and shifted in his chair, sitting back and looking at them all from a distance.

"What I'm about to tell you is beyond top secret, in fact I will authorize detention and solitary confinement for anyone found to be in breach of an utter ban in passing this information to anyone outside or this circle." He looked at all of the men around the table and lingered over Churchill trying to catch his eyes. Churchill was watching his cabinet colleagues.

Most of the men around the table shifted in their seats as Chamberlain had done. He had their attention.

"I have spoken to the King. Together we authorized a small contingent of German officials to meet with us near an airfield west of the city two days ago."

Two of the Ministers looked at each other. Two more looked down at their papers listening intently. They had all heard the rumors. Churchill stared at Chamberlain trying to read his body language. Chamberlain spoke louder than usual but sat hunched over, his gavel in hand, as if expecting to use it.

"At that meeting the Germans referenced an old treaty signed between King George III and the Holy Roman Emperor Frederick Wilhelm II which committed both sides to help each other's mutual interests. In Hampshire, the Germans suggested . . . . they proposed . . . . that we join together in a Northern Alliance, as we are both derived from the same ancient stock and think alike. They alluded to this alliance existing secretly for several centuries. What they want is to gather together an alliance of all people of northern European ancestry. They themselves are currently tied down in central Europe, surrounded by versions of themselves, which divides them into thin slices of culture, and suits no one but their enemies. They were quite open about their determination to annex all German speaking peoples and create a Greater Germany. It is really just a natural growth, a second phase if you will, after Germany was first unified by Bismarck. The next step would be a Greater Northern Europe, a joining of all the peoples with Saxon origins. They ably pointed out that we have established a Greater England and have conducted violence to achieve it. Such an Alliance would necessarily preclude any war between us and in fact give us a large say in how they conduct the creation of this Greater Anglo-Saxony. And perhaps most importantly, such an entity also serves as a bulwark against the growing threat of Communist Russia."

With that stroke, the ground had shifted beneath them all. Four of the Ministers were tongue tied, considering what they had just heard. Churchill was livid, his face red, though he breathed deeply to control his temper before he spoke.

"We have spent most of the last 400 years opposing a Greater Europe. To abandon that policy now appears short sighted. The sacrifice of hundreds of thousands of British and Empire troops in the Great War would be flushed away. I would fear a revolution here in Britain. And should this come to pass, we would be dominated as Germany has position on the continent. We would become a minor province in this new entity. This plan is just an effort to subdue us without firing a shot. And what about the French? We have already abrogated most of our obligations. An about-face on our support of France, would have implications for centuries. Think of Agincourt, Poitiers and Crecy and the generations of animosity that came from those events."

"Failure to honour our secret treaty obligations will have huge historical implications as well my dear Winston. It is time to choose," said Chamberlain. "The Germans pointed out that the French are not of the same stock as we are, and that we have been at odds with them for many centuries, as Winston has so ably pointed out, as recently as Napoleon's time or even Bismarck's. Winston, your own ancestor, the First Duke, fought the French alongside the Germanic peoples. Our co-operation with the Germans does not preclude a divorce from our French allies, in fact we might be able to convince the Germans to bring them into the fold."

"And how, pray, do the Germans propose to keep us all together when none of us trust them?"

"This is the thick of it Winston. They have suggested that our King become the King of Northern Europe and that our parliaments be integrated for transnational questions with meetings to be held in Cologne."

"And if we agree, we will be spared a bombing campaign, and perhaps an invasion?"

"Yes, yes, of course that is the gist of it."

"So we are coerced into an alliance. Do you really think that coercion will stop once we are joined?"

"The King is intrigued. His brother, Edward, has been brokering these talks."

"As much as I admire Edward he is wrong about the Nazis, they are a completely different kind of German without the honour that characterised Germans even during and after the Great War. We can never countenance this idea. It needs to be dismissed out of hand."

"Winston, haste is not wise. The idea needs to be fully considered. And frankly, if we decide not to go ahead, merely thinking on it for some months buys us time to prepare for the German response should we decline."

"On that score you are not wrong. While officially considering this we also need to understand here among us, that it will never come to pass."

"Perhaps among us only."

"A hard thing to do, as once the cat is out of the bag those in confidence will take sides and could potentially spill the plan, causing us to have to prematurely abandon it."

"And so it remains with us, and we explore it through continued meetings with the Germans. A final decision can be left until it is necessary. The Germans have requested that a delegation visit them."

"I would like us to determine our policy going forward, right now, and enshrine it into the cabinet minutes."

Chamberlain looked around the table. Nobody else spoke.

"Do I have a seconder for Mr. Churchill's motion?"

Nobody moved, save Churchill, who tried to catch the eyes of all the members of the War Cabinet.

So no vote was taken, the Cabinet tacitly agreeing with Chamberlain that a meeting would be arranged but the government would not be held to any position at that time, dragging their feet to buy time. They settled into a discussion of who their delegates should be while keeping the circle of those who knew of the nature of the situation very small.

Churchill's mind raced.

# Chapter Eight - March 1940

Churchill sat by his fish pond, which, given its size had not succumbed to the winter freeze. He thought about the fish and their journey, round and round. And thought too, about the English and their journey from a weak outpost of the Roman Empire to an Empire in her own right.

'Hitler wants the crown for credibility', he mused. 'He is obsessed with the idea that he is an upstart and not worthy to guide the German nation. For many old German families he is an Austrian, not a real German. He quickly grabbed at the Austrian crown jewels to try to gain that credibility but what he really wants is the ancient crown of the Holy Roman Emperor. Presumably he found out about it and where it had been bestowed through studying the private papers of various Prussian Kings. Or maybe Edward himself spilled the beans'. Churchill mused that Hitler probably did not know of the safe at Windsor Castle nor the keys required open it. Unless of course, Edward had tipped him off. He congratulated himself on the broader subterfuge of several researchers fanning out across Europe to hide his real intentions of searching for the keys. He mused that at some point, if Edward talked, there would be suspicions about Schroeder's research trip.

Churchill realised it was vital that the parchment treaty remain out of the hands of the Prime Minister who would use it to prop up his appeasement and sympathy for the Germans. Churchill realized that the government knew about the treaty, but the tangible papers with their official seals would lend it more credibility.

A fish breached the surface as Churchill gazed at the pond trying to ascertain the geography beneath the surface. The breach caused ripples to swell outward.

'If Hitler can get the crown, and make it known that it came to him, he can claim legitimacy as the head of the Reich and a Greater Germany. Would he honour the agreement to crown George VI? Getting that crown might lead to who knows what. He likely has designs on cementing our possible union by bestowing it on King George. Especially if he has a plan to get it back.'

Churchill had read Hitler's book, Mein Kampf, in which the German leader clearly outlined his ideas, reasons and choices. A large part of his plan was a desire to unite a Greater Germany including the almost mythical heartland of the Teutons and Saxons, lands which were for centuries Prussian and were now part of Poland. His repudiation of the Treaty of Versailles which put the blame for the Great War squarely on Germany, was visceral.

Churchill mused that Hitler wanted to greatly increase the size of Germany, first through annexation of German peoples but also by taking rich resource lands in the Carpathian Mountains and even further east into The Ukraine. The land there was not heavily populated but it was rich and fertile, exactly what a Greater Germany needed if it was to grow and prosper. Germany was industrialized but it lacked resources and farm land enough to feed the millions of a growing Germany. The Ukrainians were straining at the brutal yoke the Russians had on them and would welcome the Germans as liberators. And beyond that were the rich oil deposits of the Caucasus. Oil was now the prime mover of an industrial society and necessary to successful military action.

Churchill pondered his next move, oblivious to the chill of winter. He realized the détente of the Phony War period could not last, that spring would likely signal the next phase of the conflict.

* * * * * * * * * *

"We are growing restless and Herr Hitler's patience is thin."

Three Englishmen, two Earls and a military attaché from the Prime Minister's office, met with three German negotiators, the same three that had attended the meeting in Hampshire.

They met in Zurich, in a small hotel in the central part of the city not far from where the Limmat meets the lake, arriving separately and without informing the hotel of their event. The Germans took rooms and arranged a meeting room, while the English stayed elsewhere and slipped in one by one to avoid any attention. They avoided any uniforms and dressed as businessmen or diplomats. However, their security detail could not avoid their military bearing and subservience, obvious to anyone watching closely.

Once the group convened the Germans were quick with their accusation.

"We have intelligence which suggests you are going to invade Norway."

"And we have intelligence that you will oppose our invasion due to the questionable loyalty of one Norwegian minister."

"I may remind you gentlemen that you do not have the authorization of the Norwegian government to invade their country."

"And you have only the support of one minor Minister."

The German took a deep breath. This discussion was not moving in the direction that Hitler would have wanted and was threatening to derail the entire exercise.

"The situation in Norway is quite tense. There are several groups that would like us to intervene, including Minister Quizling's. We have held back, but an invasion by anyone without an invitation from the Norwegian government would force us to act in defence of those people who have asked for our protection of their right of self-determination."

"We can assure you if we were to go to Norway it would be with the best of intentions."

"Hrummmpphhh." The German was unimpressed. "Your assurances have not had much value in the past, so my Czech, Polish and French friends tell me."

"Certainly the Norwegians would be included in a Northern Kingdom?"

"Which is a reason we would respond to their pleas for help."

"Well yes, quite. We are here to talk about your proposal, not some imagined military actions in Scandinavia. And on that, we are still looking for assurances."

"You have them. We have not engaged in any offensive operations for the entire fall of 1939 and winter of 1940. We will not wait forever. We understand that this delay is allowing the French to bolster their munitions and ranks. The Russians appear daily less likely to remain in our alliance. Any delay is a threat. We require an answer to our proposal of unity."

"I will take your concerns back to the Prime Minister and he will issue an announcement once he has had time to consider all the implications."

* * * * * * * * * *

May Day in London was a festive time. The deepening of Spring with daily hints of the Summer to come gave everyone an optimistic view. The British war cabinet met after minutes of the Swiss meeting were circulated among them.

"The Germans are pressing. They demand an answer," Chamberlain intoned.

"We cannot do this. Not with the duplicity of Norway so fresh."

English troops had landed in Norway to oppose Germans bent on exercising their power to control the country after one faction of the Norwegian government invited them in. A few skirmishes and some jockeying combined with a lack of strong support from any faction of the erstwhile Norwegian government, and the British evacuated, unwilling to spark combat and scuttle the unity talks. Tensions were boiling but full scale war had remained in check. The Germans had acted but remained unwilling to take on the British directly, content to show their position on the ground and keep the British from escalating the conflict due to poor position, supplies and logistical support.

"And yet we need to find some way to deny the idea while still keeping it open."

The denial of an immediate move to reinforce the Union plan and a request for more meetings were communicated to the German high command on May 5. The denial of the basic plan included several logistical issues, such as the location of joint parliamentary meetings, the crowning of King George, and the tentative steps to integrate the militaries, trade, and currency issues. These items were necessary to finding a way forward, and so the British argued that more time and meetings were required.

The German ambassador communicated that an announcement of the Union was necessary within 48 hours, and that details could be worked out after that step had been taken.

The British asked after possible meeting times.

Three days later the Germans began their attack upon France, rolling through the Ardennes Forest in Belgium along the French border, much as Churchill had predicted. French resistance collapsed along the lightly defended area.

"Well, it appears as if our decision on unity has been made," said Chamberlain. "Without defences in the Ardennes quarter, the French were simply outflanked."

"It's the same thing the German's did to them in 1870 and again in 1914. It is necessary to defend the entire border, even if a border region is with a non-belligerent. The Germans simply invaded Belgium on their way to Paris. How is it possible to be so foolish? These are our allies, who we are counting on."

"Somehow the French have a history of disastrous military efforts and yet they still exist as a nation. Save for a few tactical innovations by Napoleon and the joie de vie of Joan of Arc, what military successes have the French had?"

"Theirs is a lesson on the power of language and history to keep a culture alive."

Within days the Germans had captured thousands of French troops and swung their Panzers west and north to trap the British Army and retreating portions of the French and Belgian armies.

Chamberlain's government fell. For years it had been a group of mewling antiwar pacifists, infiltrated by a number of virtual Nazis, or at least German sympathizers who sided with the stern policies of the Fascists or outright supported their fanatic extremism.

The folly of Chamberlain's pacifism was laid bare, he was forced to resign and in the end handed the reins of power to Churchill, recommending that King George appoint him over any rivals. The swift invasion of France seemed to cast doubt on German promises to consider the issue of eventually bringing the French into an alliance, save by force.

Churchill took the reins of government and made his first priority regrouping the British by getting them off the Channel Beaches.

"This was inevitable Winston. We managed to buy time, but not enough. The British Army will be slaughtered in the tens of thousands along with any French who remain."

"Get the men off the French beaches by any means possible."

Winston made frantic calls to anyone with a boat and begged them to sail the Channel and get as many people and as much equipment out of France while they could. The British high command hoped to get 40,000 men out of harm's way before the Germans sealed off their escape. The operation was slow, doomed it seemed to the amount of time necessary to ferry men off the beach in small craft to larger ships a few miles out to sea. The larger ships could not get too close to the coastline. They were under fire, though their distances from the coast gave them a measure of protection.

"The Germans will not answer to your calls for more discussion. They have called us duplicitous."

"Offer them the crown."

"I'm not sure what you mean. I imagine King George might object."

"Not that crown. Offer them the Holy Ro . . . the Austrian crown. They know by now that we have it and Hitler covets it. Offer them the crown for a few days grace to evacuate France."

"It seems a high price to pay for only a few days."

"It's just a metal circlet. Hitler wants to reunite it with the Austrian Crown jewels. It's just a metal circle and well worth the lives of thousands of men, if we can get them off the Coast."

The Foreign Office official returned to Churchill two hours later.

"They have accepted your deal. Five days grace, but if they do not receive the crown within 24 hours they will not honour the agreement. And they want you to deliver it personally."

"Their honour has always been in question. Let them know we will deliver the crown within 24 hours. Our man will be in Amiens Cathedral where he will hand it over. They can get delivery from him. Do not refer to the five days they offered, only reference getting our people off the Beach, perhaps that will buy us a bit more time. And then they will come, and they will visit violence upon our shores. We will have the Channel between us and a sliver of hope."

The evacuation stepped up. Surely not all Germans had been told to stand down as some sorties, particularly by the Luftwaffe, hampered efforts.

An aide poked his head into Churchill's study at No. 10 Downing Street. He had only been named Prime Minister a few days before so the study was still awaiting its full Churchillian make over, with items stacked and spread out from the desk, but not yet completely filling the room. Some of Chamberlain's personal items had been packed into boxes stacked against one wall.

"It appears Hitler has held back as the mechanized armies have stopped. We are still being harassed by planes and our troops are fighting back. The Luftwaffe has not been informed or is ignoring the orders. Hitler has turned his interests toward Paris. It appears that he understands if our troops are evacuated he no longer has to worry about them."

"Hitler has said he will hold off but not stop until the crown is delivered. It will take a few days to get these men off the beaches."

Churchill nodded, dismissed the aide and lifted the telephone receiver.

* * * * * * * * * *

"Professor Schroeder, there is an urgent message for you, I hope everything is alright."

Schroeder stopped his lecture. He looked at the messenger at the door and then back to the students listening intently. He met the messenger half way and accepted the sealed paper. It bore no marks save for his name and a very crudely drawn small circle with a narrow slit in its center and a crudely drawn key to one side.

He resisted the desire to tear it open and ignored the raised eyebrows of his students when he failed to open it. He completed the lecture, only once stumbling as his thoughts about the message overtook his planned talk.

He left the lecture hall and made for his office. He feared that the message was to hide himself in the face of threats from German or possibly Russian agents. Once the door closed he tore open the page and read . . .

"Prof. Schroeder, I have a favour to ask. It is at the utmost urgency that I need a delivery made to Amiens Cathedral, tomorrow morning. You will be delivered to Dieppe at dawn, met by car and driven to Amiens where you are to deliver a parcel. Then you will come home by the same means, and should be back in your office by supper time. Please call this number immediately, able or no."

He thought a moment and dialed.

"Hello Schroeder."

"Sir Winston, how did you know it was me?"

"It was either you or my wife, no one else has this number. And since my wife is out of town, I expected you."

"I am reluctant to continue in this work. I am too nervous and frankly frightened. What am I to deliver?"

"The crown. Charlemagne's crown. That is what was in the box your keys opened. In short, Hitler wants it, and has pledged to cease fire for several days while we collect men off the French Beaches. Thousands will die if we do not get this artifact to him quickly. They have ceased their encirclement but are still harassing the troops, including French and Belgian armies, with an air campaign."

Schroeder felt himself go weak in the knees and his head began to swim.

"Schroeder, Schroeder?"

"Yes, Sir Winston, can you not get anyone else?"

"I could but that means letting more people in on the secret."

Schroeder thought a moment, "It's just a delivery? When do I leave."

"One hour. You will be picked up your residence by taxi. One of ours. The car will drive you to Portsmouth. There you will pick up the package and receive a quick briefing. There will be more details of the delivery available in Portsmouth."

"Okay. Thanks. I don't mean 'thanks' exactly."

"I do thank you. One of your assignments will be to examine the crown thoroughly while enroute. We don't expect anything unusual but we leave nothing to chance. And you speak their language and the language of Amiens and Dieppe."

Schroeder thought, there would be no opportunity to tell Anderson of his mission, he only hoped that Anderson did not come looking for him this night. He did not want to lie to his American friends. Would the Germans be surprised to see him? He had never acted on their proposal and wanted to keep his distance. He was not comfortable with the cloak and dagger and did not want complications.

He made his way home by the usual route, unusually wary of everything around him.

It was not yet dark when a black taxi glided up to his home in Ealing an hour later. He walked out to meet the car carrying nothing, as if he would be returning forthwith.

The street was quiet but the taxi and its passenger were noted.

The driver acknowledged him by name only and said their trip would take about two hours. Something to eat would be available upon arrival in Portsmouth.

Schroeder was sitting on the edge of his seat to better hear the driver when he straightened his back and slid deep into the bench, head up but thinking of nothing concrete. He was familiar with Portsmouth, the Channel, Dieppe and Amiens but in every other way he was headed deeply into the unknown.

# Chapter Nine

At Portsmouth the taxi passed a checkpoint and stopped just inside a guarded perimeter beside a concrete block building, shored up with sandbags. Schroeder was whisked inside and guided quickly into a small conference room, feeling more a prisoner than a free man. Winston sat drinking tea.

"Thank you Professor Schroeder for taking on this assignment." The newly minted Prime Minister produced a pair of 8 x 10 glossy photos.

"These are the two men you are to meet. They are known German agents and will take the package from you, at which point your job is complete and you can return to England by reversing the course on which you arrived in Amiens."

Both photographed men were plain looking, vaguely clean shaven, short haired and a bit grubby. They looked like working men at the end of a long shift.

"These men will have a fleur-dys-lis pin on their lapels and you are to wear your wrist watch on your right wrist. Make sure it can be seen. You also must wear this scarf loosely around your neck but under your coat," Churchill handed him a crimson scarf. "Speak to them first in English saying, 'The church is not too crowded today.' They will reply, 'No, it is usually much busier.' Hand them this case and you can leave. That is the official version of our agreed arrangements. I also want you to tell them that if they do not honour our agreement, and attack our men in France or try to invade Britain, the Americans have agreed to come to our defence and will immediately declare war on them."

Schroeder nodded.

"It is now 9:47 pm. It will take you an hour to cross the channel. You will be delivered into Dieppe in the morning. You will meet a car at Eglise St. Jacques and will be driven for 75 minutes until you reach Amiens Cathedral. Your arrival there is slated for 8:40 a.m. Finding your contacts and making the transaction should take less than 10 minutes. You are to reverse course. The car will be waiting where it dropped you. You will head back to Dieppe and should be back in London for supper. We will conduct a short debriefing upon your return to Portsmouth. You will leave here at 5:45 a.m. You will be roused at 4:30 a.m. and given a bite to eat and then the mission will commence. Thank you on behalf of the Crown and the Empire."

Schroeder nodded again. There did not seem much to say.

He slept fitfully in a chair. Roused at 4:30 a.m. as promised, he readied himself for the trip, not wanting to take much sustenance in case there were rough seas in the Channel. More than once he had made that mistake and a quick 45 minute trip had turned into a nightmare of nausea, spread across several hours, as ferry boats fought the weather.

He was directed out the back of the block building and taken by a small shuttle car to an empty dock a bit more than a quarter mile away.

"I expected the boat would be waiting for us," said aloud.

"It is." They pulled up to the edge of the jetty and down, hugging the water was a submarine. There was a staircase down to a fixed walkway and a movable ramp which ended where a hatch was open, awaiting its passenger.

"Oh. I suppose I should have expected this."

"It's wartime mate. You thought perhaps we'd run you across on the Queen Mary?"

Schroeder had to smile to himself.

"Okay. So how do I get off."

"Four of our boys are going to row you in from about a half mile out, just south of the harbour. You will land among some fishing boats and while they take charge of the boat you make your way to the center of town. The taxi is waiting for you to the west of St. Jacques and you are to ask the driver if he is engaged. He will answer, 'No, I'm already married.' All in English. You are to laugh."

Schroeder followed the attendant down the staircase, across the walkway and down the moveable stair and onto a small deck adjacent to the hatch. He found his way down a ladder and stood facing the submarine's captain, who saluted him. He hesitated and then weakly returned the salute, saying, "Sorry, I'm not military."

"Quite alright Sir, force of habit, don't you know."

They descended into the sub, the Captain gave the signal to seal the hatch, and loudly spoke a series of orders to back the sub away from the dock. Those orders were repeated back to him from a distance. The submarine immediately dropped under the surface as it turned into the harbour and moved at speed into the

Channel. The Captain directed Schroeder into a sitting room and joined him with some small talk.

"This mission was unexpected, though it's something we are trained for. It came from the Admiralty, but not through the usual channels. However, if I'm not to know any details, then please do not divulge them."

The captain arranged for a bite to eat and any other creature comforts that Schroeder requested, eventually receiving a signal that they were about to surface and move their cargo. Alone during that time Schroeder opened the small case to look at the circlet. He noted the slightly crude nature of the forging and setting of the ruby as well as the gem's slightly misshapen cut. He thoroughly inspected the entire piece and saw a tiny inscription on the inside of the band but he could not make out its meaning. Only a few letters in length it looked like a few Latin words or initials of an inscription but not one with which he was familiar. It was followed by the letters DCCC.

Schroeder made note of what he saw and placed the band back in the case before taking a cup of tea and a scone as the submarine was travelling quite smoothly under the waves. It did not take long before Schroeder was directed up the ladder as the hatch was opened above him. As he emerged he was able to feel the swells of the waves, but upon reaching the top of the hatch he noticed the sea was fairly calm. The visual of calm helped his nerves but he still made an effort to avoid any feelings of nausea caused by the sub's motion on the surface. There was a barely perceptible back and forth motion as the submarine was hit by each wave and a corresponding up and down motion as it rode the swells.

"This is the closest we can get in deep water. Be safe, but be quick. We do not want to linger and can only remain submerged for so long."

Four burly sailors had scrambled up the ladder ahead of him and as he emerged he saw a small craft, very low in the water, which had apparently been lashed to the side of the submarine, and was now readied for his journey.

He was the last aboard and the craft was released from its tether to the submarine and the men began to row with conviction toward the shore, aiming for a spot just south of the harbour entrance. Looking back he saw that the sub had quickly disappeared below the waves.

The small boat beached and Schroeder was quickly sent on his way as the rowers took charge of their vessel. Having been provided with directions to the Church of St. Jacques a few blocks away, he could already see the spire of the ancient church. As he stepped up the stone sea wall he looked back to see the men pulling the boat up on the beach. They flipped it over and one man remained with it to insure it would still be there. The rest dispersed but would remain within sight of the small craft and could be down the beach and away in minutes once they received the signal that Schroeder had returned.

Still in unoccupied France, Schroeder was cautious but not afraid. He was more concerned with officials witnessing his strange entrance into the country than he was about anything else. A few blocks into the city he blended in with inhabitants beginning their day.

At the church, he circled it and found a taxi waiting along one side of the large building. Following the protocols he had been taught he found the driver and gave the required response. With the necessary laugh and a smirk of success he got in the car and it moved off quickly. The driver said nothing more until they entered the city limits of Amiens.

"There in about 15 minutes. I will park and be waiting in the same space. There is place for standing taxis."

Minutes later Schroeder got out of the car, took note of the taxi and moved up the steps to the cathedral's eastern entrance and went inside without looking back. Immediately the stone of the church turned the air cool. His eyes adjusted to the low light and he began to circle the building, wandering down one of the transepts along the nave and watching carefully all the movement in the building. He doubled back and crossed the front entrance portico and moved up the outside aisle toward the crossing. Still some distance away he saw a man standing near the choir reading a plaque. He looked like a working man and as Schroeder approached he was joined by a second man, similarly dressed. The second man was more distinctive in appearance with a small moustache and a thick wave of hair above his eyes. He looked quintessentially French. As Schroeder moved past them he noticed a fleur-dys-lis pin on one lapel.

"Escuse-moi," he said. "The church is not too crowded today."

The man with the lapel pin looked startled. "No, it is usually much busier." He looked pointedly at Schroeder's lapels and then glanced down at Schroeder's right arm.

Schroeder nodded slightly and held out the small case he held. The man took it and made to leave but Schroeder stopped him.

"I am also to tell you, that should you fail to honour our agreement, the Americans will declare against you."

The man's eyes grew large. He had already partly turned away as Schroeder spoke and he finished his turn and started walking towards the west door, closest to their location near the choir. The second man walked quickly, almost galloping to keep up.

Schroeder could not help but look around him, his mission essentially complete. He felt entirely conspicuous but no one seemed to be paying him any attention. He pretended to read the plaque briefly and then slowly walked across the front of the choir and out the east side door to where his taxi was waiting.

As he emerged into the bright sun, he waited a moment to allow his eyes to adjust and he moved down the large stone staircase towards the taxi stand. There was only one car there, and it matched his own, with a Dieppe Taxi sign on its roof. He entered the car quickly. There was someone already sitting in it behind the driver, and as he sat down, the locks clicked closed and the car moved away from the curb.

"Herr Schroeder," said a middle aged man dressed in a dark suit. "The Fuhrer is pleased with your work. Don't worry we are on our way back to Dieppe. Herr Hitler has another assignment for you."

"Major? Major Kilhofer? Sir, I have only just visited the Cathedral. Evidently you know much of my business."

"The Fuhrer wants you to perform one more little mission."

"But I haven't performed any yet."

"Oh, but you have Herr Schroeder. And now the most important one. You must ensure that the Americans do not enter the war. For our part we do not want to attack Britain, but we will if pushed. A message if you will to Churchill."

"But Herr Kilhofer, my message from Churchill was that should you fail in your side of the agreement the Americans will declare war against you. It seems both sides do not want to be pushed."

"Herr Hitler is looking for signs of agreement. However, belligerence, and attempting to bring the Americans into negotiations of our joint reorganization of Europe will not be received well. Should Churchill remain belligerent we will be forced to show Englanders what we can do."

"Churchill is steadfast. He does not trust Hitler and he stands by

British policy of opposing anyone on the continent who threatens to become too powerful."

The car wound its way through some of the outer streets of Amiens, evidently headed west to Dieppe.

"That is not news Herr Schroeder. It is up to you to convey our intentions. And frankly should that fail, we will ask you to kill Winston Churchill, as you have access to him. The Fuhrer will stand at nothing to bring about a Greater Germany."

Schroeder was shaking. He was no spy but had somehow gotten entangled far beyond his ability to disengage. He was determined to disentangle himself.

"I am an American, sir."

"And as such we can visit your family, should we need to. You will be provided with instructions on how to remove Churchill should it come to that. Our man's code name is 'Frederick the Great'. An escape back to Germany can be arranged with a prestigious chair at a leading university, under an assumed name."

Schroeder was silent, contemplating his options.

"I am no spy sir. I merely did what I was asked to save men trying to escape to Great Britain."

"Perhaps not, but you have become one and perhaps also an assassin, should Churchill fail to come to terms."

The car was a few blocks from the Church of St. Jacques. The door locks clicked open.

"Return to England. We will be in touch."

And with that Kilhofer offered his hand to Schroeder to shake. He did so unwillingly, weakly, as shaking his hand seemed to bind him to Kilhofer's proposals.

Schroeder felt a piece of paper in his fist. He got out and tried to avoid looking at his hand. Before he could turn away from the taxi it left him, moving at speed quickly around a corner as if it had never been there.

Schroeder turned away, determined not to look in his hand until he was some distance away. It was not implausible he thought, that the Germans had been informed who would make the delivery, so they engaged Kilhofer to meet him, to add weight to their proposal. Considering these things he took a deep breath, eyeing the buildings around him to get his bearings, and started back to the waterfront, sliding his hand into his jacket pocket. He descended the steps down the seawall to the beach and saw three men making their way towards him. One pointed away left where another man was turning over the small boat and tossing oars into it.

They all converged and quickly began to pull the boat toward the water, pushing it in and away from the beach as one by one they jumped into the boat and began to row away from shore. A few beachcombers watched them with curiosity as such exits from the beach were rare. Usually boats of any kind left from the harbour, though the boat was so small it attracted little consideration as locals thought maybe it was just members of a rowing club, though curiously dressed for such an occasion.

"All is well sir?"

Schroeder was silent. He nodded but remained deep in thought, finally dipping his hand into his jacket pocket to make sure the slip of paper was still there. He was even more determined to come clean with both his American friends who might warn his family, and with Churchill who he saw as a bulwark against a tyranny he had not really contemplated. He had not expected Major Kilhofer, even though the driver was the same man. 'A double agent? He must have heard Kilhofer. Who was in league with who?' he wondered.

They rowed for 25 minutes, and continued as they waited for the submarine to surface.

"We are to meet it further out as it will likely be seen closer to shore in the full light of day."

"There, there is the periscope. They are looking for us."

"And they scan the surface to see if the coast is clear."

There were no ships near them and only a few fishing vessels could be seen several miles to the north east.

The periscope moved toward them slowly. One of the men lashed a rope around it and gave a thumbs up into the glass viewfinder.

The rope tightened against the gunwale of the small boat and it began to make a low wake in the water despite the medium swells of the sea.

They were pulled for several miles to the west before the periscope did a complete circle and the submarine surfaced. The hatch opened and the men scrambled into the ship, the small boat was reattached to the outside of the submarine as the larger boat moved north at a stately pace, a look out ready to signal the captain should there be any need to submerge.

"Mission accomplished, sir?"

Schroeder made a wan smile, "Yes captain. Everything went according to plan."

The captain nodded and turned to leave the sitting room, telling Schroeder they would be at Portsmouth within 45 minutes.

Once out of the room the captain met with the rowing men.

"It appears to have been a text book operation lads."

"Yes, yes it does. However, Lenny was on hand at St. Jacques when our man returned. He was not alone."

"Not alone?"

"Well, I was making my way to the church to observe when the cab passed me on the street. There were definitely two people in the back. I scrambled to follow and our man emerged about a block on, still a little way from the church. The taxi had the same markings, the same cab number on the sign, though the driver never got out, he appeared to be our man, or at least looked like him. The taxi disappeared before I could get a good look."

The sub arrived back at Portsmouth and Schroeder was taken into a conference room.

A military man joined him.

"Mr. Schroeder, the mission was a success?"

"Well, I suppose. I delivered the package as planned with the appropriate words and warnings I was asked to convey."

"But there is more too it?"

"Well yes. Am I authorized to speak to you of it?"

The Captain mused a second, "Yes, they wanted me to ascertain your immediate impressions, though there will be a fully debrief at Portsmouth."

"First, the man taking the package seemed awfully surprised when I added the caveat of the consequences should they potentially break the agreement. I went immediately to meet the cab and it was the only one in the taxi stand. I got in but I was not alone."

The military man looked at another man who was taking notes.

"They seemed to know about me, and asked that I deliver a message back to Churchill. They said if Churchill is belligerent they will be forced to show us what they can do."

"Anything else?"

"Yes, they said they knew of my family in America and asked that I do their bidding. An obvious attempt to coerce me into agreeing."

"And did you?"

"What agree? No, I told them I was no spy. They disagreed. They offered me an escape and a university chair in Germany if I co-operated with them."

Everything Schroeder said was written down and double checked and he was asked multiple times if there was anything more he could add. They wanted the smallest detail while it was fresh in his mind and did not stop him when he recollected things that were obviously not related.

"Our man Schroeder has a bit of a photographic memory."

"Indeed, simply press him and he remembers astonishing detail on buildings, people walking by, signs and the like and he wasn't even trying to remember these things when they occurred."

Schroeder was run through the same questions upon arriving at the naval base and then taken home by car, a nearby resident noting his arrival. After a time he decided to make his way to the local pub. Sure enough his friend Anderson was there and saddled up beside him.

"You didn't go home last night."

"Well I did but I left late and stayed away for the night as I could not get back easily. Truth is I was asked to deliver a message to the Germans in France, to the effect that if Britain was not allowed to get its men and material off the beaches at Dunkirk, the Americans would enter the war on the British side."

"News to me, but they don't tell me everything."

"The Germans want me to turn and help them spy on Churchill, and perhaps assassinate him at some point. They threatened my family in Pennsylvania should I fail to side with them."

"So they admit to having agents in the States, I suppose that isn't a surprise. Surely you didn't travel all the way to France to speak with them, that could have been accomplished by wireless?"

"Churchill also asked me to drop them a package - about the size of a breadbox but only a slice of one, not nearly so wide, but I don't know what was in the box."

"You didn't look?"

"It was sealed. And frankly I don't want to know. I am not a spy, just a messenger."

"We are going to have to do something to protect your family, unless of course you are going to kill Churchill."

Schroeder gave Anderson a long look. "I'm done with this business. I hate it all. I just want to go back to my students, my books and my work."

"We are working out a new contact, even though I will still visit with you here. The Brits are on to us so we have to play it up, but if you get anything more substantial you and I can arrange for a more secure drop."

"I told you I am done. Look, I'm happy to speak with you, and help out the cause and all. The Brits know about this so who cares. But I am done. I can't handle the pressure."

Anderson shrugged. "Which means you are still in, even if you have one foot on the outside. Let me think on the best way to protect you from the Germans." And with that he drained his pint, slid off the high stool and took his leave.

Schroeder sat there thinking. He absentmindedly ordered another pint, again with the sliver of ice added. He poured the last bit of his first pint into the second and pushed the empty glass away from the edge of the bar. He could not focus on what had happened to him nor how it would affect him going forward. Major Kilhofer's presence meant something, but he did not know what. As he reached into his pocket to pay for the pints he felt the slip of paper, forgotten in the scramble to return to England. He pulled it out and read, 'I am a member of an underground group opposed to Hitler. Please help me if I ask, and I will help you.'

Schroeder was thunderstruck. Was this message a ruse? Was Kilhofer for real or was he trying to drag him into some nefarious plot? The complications were so thick that Schroeder did not know what to believe.

He decided to listen to news reports or anything in the papers that pointed to the apparent agreement that Churchill had with Hitler. But there was nothing. Anderson appeared legitimate and Churchill had so far been honest with him. Everything else was a jumble.

The next several days confirmed that the agreement between Churchill and Hitler had held. While it was never spoken about or written in the news too specifically, it was obvious to anyone reading between the lines that the British had escaped France by the skin of their teeth. Hundreds of thousands of British and French troops were hastily put up in armed camps all around London. The return of 40,000 men that had been considered their best hope, swelled into 340,000 men removed from the Beaches near Dunkirk. It did not escape Schroeder that with the return of British forces the Nazis did not have to house them as prisoners of war and they had removed the bulk of opposition to their push on Paris.

Fortunate for this mass of humanity, the late spring weather was conducive to light shelters. More substantial housing would be needed come autumn. Yet another logistical concern with Britain on the brink of hostilities.

Trickles of news about engagements in Scandinavia had reached the public with the War Department crowing about some successes and burying their retreat as the Nazis swarmed Norway.

Once the men were safe there had been occasional bombing runs into Britain but they were small and targeted to munitions and military. Almost as if Hitler signalled his willingness to engage the British while still holding out hope for a truce and perhaps more. With the fall of France bombers slowly stepped up their campaign, but no invasion force materialized on English beaches.

But by September, with no further contact from Britain on any alliance, Hitler's attitude changed and the huge air raids began with bombing becoming indiscriminate. They were terror raids really, with whole neighbourhoods wiped out on a nightly basis. Air raids, battles to push the bombers away and an ever increasing civil defence strategy, with blackouts, volunteer fire brigades, and people sheltering in subway stations, pushed the war into an everyday fear.

On radio Churchill stoked the fear calling for measures to be taken should an invasion force land upon Britain's shores. In the south and east directional signs were taken down or reversed. Signs for town names were switched out. Anything to confuse an invasion force. And coastal defenses were beefed up.

The British bore up as well as might be expected and the tactics they used resonated through the decades, as children were billeted into families in the country, ancient manor homes were used to house displaced people, neighbourhoods were remade and many of London's remaining medieval buildings, those that survived the Great Fire of 1666, were blown to oblivion.

As Schroeder walked home one evening Alexi fell into step with him.

"Professor, we need you to deliver a message."

Anderson visited him in the pub one night.

"Your family has been moved and their names changed." He pushed a piece of paper to Schroeder. It contained several names and an address in Texas. "Your father was reluctant but in the end we convinced him. He did not believe that the Germans were capable of such brutality."

"A Russian agent spoke to me last night. He wants me to deliver a message."

"That cements it. Christoph we believe you should be disappeared. If you want out, then I can arrange for you to go back to the States, with a name change and a job at a small college. I suggest we arrange an accidental death, say a traffic accident. If the Germans believed you dead they are less likely to pursue your family."

Schroeder asked for time to think on it. Churchill had made a similar proposal. He was inclined to accept the American offer but actually follow through with the British offer so he could remain in Britain. What was necessary was a co-ordination of the circumstances. He had a strong feeling that if the Americans thought him dead he might be better off.

Anderson left. Sitting in the pub he mused on the facts of the situation as he knew them. And what struck him was there were very few actual, unassailable facts on which to hang any truth.

He was in the sights of all belligerents. They were all playing him for their own ends. He wanted to remain in Britain from a professional standpoint. Kilhofer was a member of the underground? Or was he playing a part? Alexi wanted him to help but never actually asked anything of him. Churchill kept using his services but must have access to many more experienced people. Anderson seemed legitimate and was happy to keep him engaged.

'So what is truth? An amalgam of facts, presumably. But whose facts?' He tried to think everything through.

'To scholars, facts in a book carry weight, but why? Presumably because they have been vetted by the publisher, a third party. But it is obvious that something printed in a book is not necessarily a fact. So what is a fact? What is truth?'

'This notion of facts being agreed upon nuggets of truth, is a broad definition but not one that stands up to scrutiny. Some widely agreed upon 'facts' are simply not true. And, some things that are not widely agreed upon, are true.'

'Truth is not an opinion on fact. It is not a popularity contest. Truth, real truth is unambiguous, unassailable. But, if that is the case, real truth is largely inaccessible as even the most unambiguous and unassailable thing you can think of, includes an exception, a circumstance where it is clearly not applicable.'

'Truth therefore must be personal. Your truth, your deep seated belief is just as true to you as mine is to me. The difficulty is living with that conundrum and being comfortable within it. Once the ability to leave room for doubt or an alternative interpretation of apparent facts is gone, then you have fascism, a totalitarian demand for conformity that is essentially non-human.'

And with that Schroeder drained his pint and made to leave. He was no closer to understanding what was happening but he did feel better with the belief that no one else knew anything more.

# Chapter Ten - July 1941

"Churchill wants me to deliver another message in France. He is proposing I go to Biarritz by sea and make my way to Switzerland, all to deliver a message."

"What on Earth for?"

"He says he has a message and a package that needs to be delivered. Can you arrange for me to be disappeared once I am there? Preferably on my way back, so Churchill is satisfied the message was successfully delivered? I would like to return to the States after this mission."

Anderson sat without saying anything. He waited a time, thinking, and then slowly nodded.

"So who are you delivering the message to?"

"I am to meet with a representative of the German High Command."

They met again a few days later. Anderson gave Schroeder two letters.

"We need you to deliver this to members of the underground in occupied France. Our normal channels of communications have been broken and this information should help restore it. Once done you will be met by some of our agents in Le Puy, a town in central France, and diverted away from the British plan for your return. We will escort you south to Portugal and then back to the US. To the Brits the Germans and the Russians you will go missing but will be free of your obligations and baggage. We have secured you a professorship at a private California university with an assumed name and history."

Schroeder nodded. Anderson flipped open a map of France and pointed out Le Puy En Velay, and the likely route he would be taking from Switzerland to get there.

Schroeder passed this information on to Churchill.

"Perfect Professor Schroeder, just like our American friends to wrap it all up so neatly. "

Familiar with the method of entering France, Schroeder was ferried into Biarritz, and spirited across France into Switzerland, handed from one underground contact to the next.

Travelling from safe house to safe house across central France Schroeder was able to deliver Anderson's envelope. The new government in this part of France was beholden to their Nazi supporters and unreliable to the Allied cause. However some members of that government were involved in the underground resistance. Beholden to the Nazis they walked on eggshells in constant fear of local reprisals or a general take over by German forces. They were watched carefully by Nazi minders and given tasks to constantly check their loyalty. Among them was the search for Jews.

Schroeder dropped the note from Anderson at a small house in Vichy, and instructed the receiver to meet him in a nearby park in

15 minutes if there was a message to go back.

Sure enough, about 10 minutes later a man strolled into the park with a dog. Schroeder sat on a bench very close to the end of his patience.

"Your note?" he asked. Schroeder nodded.

"I will do what I can to help. We need new radio transmitters. Have the underground contact me. Code word, 'papillion verte' and the return phrase, 'There are many such butterflies in the Vichy area.' I am not sure of my abilities but I will try. I will pass on the information in your note about the drop zone for supplies."

Schroeder had been scratching the dog under its chin and smiling while constantly shifting his eyes for any indication they were being watched.

He rose, saluted the dog and bid farewell to its master and turned from the park where he was met upon exit with his resistance minder anxious to continue his trip to Switzerland.

"And now, we need to find M. Cattalone so I can deliver this letter."

"As I mentioned no one here has heard of such a person but our group is looking, especially in this area, where you say he should be."

A day later and news came that M. Cattalone was found and was known to the group by another name.

"He was most frightened when our man asked him if Cattalone was his name. He's a farmer outside of town. We have used his farm as a safe house, as approaches there are visible for quite a distance."

Schroeder was hidden in a vegetable cart and taken to M. Cattalone's farm that evening.

The expat American delivered his letter from Anderson and he left having decided to use darkness to travel to Grenoble.

In Grenoble he arranged with the underground to help him cross into Switzerland, and once inside, he made his way across that country without difficulty. At the border with Austria he made no attempt to hide who he was, saying he was an envoy from England and was expected to deliver a message and letter into the hand of the German High Command at Salzburg. The border guards made him wait, and he was fetched by a German officer and driven into the Austrian Tyrol and eventually to a small town south of Salzburg. He couldn't quite put a label on his status. Sometimes he seemed a captive, sometimes an official envoy, or an underground messenger and finally almost as an ambassador.

"Why can't you simply deliver my message to your superior officers?"

"We are. We are just delivering you to them as well, at their request."

After an anxious night in a hotel in town, a large staff car rolled up in the morning and Schroeder was directed inside. As he got into the back a Nazi officer joined him.

"Hello again Professor Schroeder. It seems you have risen in the ranks of the Foreign Office and are no longer just an academic doing research."

Major Franz Kilhofer smiled a crooked smile as the car smoothly whisked Schroeder through town. The small settlement was striking as it was built along the lower folds of the mountains, with roadways following the tops of deep ravines and large homes sitting on the higher slopes. It looked to Schroeder as if it was an enclave of wealth and privilege far off the common routes of travel.

"Major, I was tasked by British Prime Minister Winston Churchill with delivering a message to your senior command. I expect because I speak German and have had some experience with German officials in the new regime. Sadly it has taken much time away from my writing pursuits. I had gathered quite a bit of research together on my last visit and have put it into some form. I have had two shorter articles published about my findings but the real writing of the book length piece has only just begun."

"You appear to be Churchill's private envoy given your delivery to Amiens a few month ago."

"Ah, that. Again, speaking German is an advantage."

"You were in France."

"I suppose I was, but I speak French as well, and given the circumstances having a multilingual messenger was seen as an advantage. Believe me when I say, I am not cut out for this stuff. I prefer my quiet life and a classroom of semi-interested students. However, it is difficult to say 'No' to Churchill."

The large staff car was gliding up a steep slope now that they had left the settled area behind. Eventually they turned off the main road and passed a sentry point just a short distance up the sloping roadway. This lonely road angled deeper into the forest and soon began an assent to a higher elevation, winding up the side of a small mountain with a few switchbacks along the way. The car eventually reached the end of the road at a sheer rock face with a significant portion of the mountain still looming above them. With a wave from the driver, a large rolling door rose up and the car glided into the mountain, driving on into the tunnel for about 100 yards. At the end was a space easily wide enough to turn a car around. Several large black staff cars were parked along one wall. Exposed ventilation ducts ran across the high ceiling. Hewn rock was visible between the structural reinforcements.

Schroeder's door was opened and as he stood up two uniformed guards stepped out of the shadows to check him over. A few questions and a quick pat down and the party was moved through a double door into a small room where one of several other doors slid open with a mechanical sound revealing an elevator car. Kilhofer remained behind. Anderson was mildly surprised when the car rose, rather than fell into what he expected was a fortified bunker. After 30 seconds the doors opened up on a large high ceilinged room fitted out in pine and filled with light. Exiting the elevator, uniformed SS men patted Schroder down again and gave his two guards a cursory inspection.

They walked up a short curved staircase following the contour of the wall which at the top opened on a huge room, outfitted in wood with a pine ceiling and a glass wall at the far side. There were several passageways from the room and a short staircase leading up at one end. Glass separated the large indoor sitting room, an elegant chalet really, with plush chairs, couches and low tables; from a wide and lengthy balcony with a stone floor, framed by a waist high stone wall. Beyond that wall was a sheer drop and the stunning vista of the Austrian Alps. The mountains were still capped with snow but the spring temperatures had melted the snow blankets of the trees. Behind the nearest initial crest of peaks, the mountains marched on into the distance like rippling waves, with crest after crest receding into the distance. Their snowy tops made them look like whitecaps on a churning sea.

Schroeder gasped audibly.

And silhouetted against the glass wall a voice said in German, "Welcome Herr Schroeder, I am gratified you are impressed. Welcome to the Eagle's Nest."

He was waved toward the balcony, through a doorway in the glass, escorted by the man who had welcomed him. Still barely able to keep his eyes off the scenery, Schroeder was directed to a chair where he settled down. He looked about and stared in amazement at Adolph Hitler, dressed in a dark business suit standing a few feet away.

Schroeder was stunned. He leaped up and stammered a hello and self-introduction. He had been expecting to meet with a high ranking military man even after seeing the view. This was no secure military stronghold, this was a pleasure spot designed to inspire awe.

Hitler extended his hand and with a smile greeted Schroeder in German. A translator began to render the greeting into English but Schroeder spoke, returning the greeting in German.

"Herr Hitler," he said with a slight bow from the neck, his heels coming together inadvertently, "I am most impressed with this place. However, I expected to deliver my message quickly and be gone. I am very uncomfortable with this kind of work. I am just a Professor of History, and social history at that, rather than military or political."

"Herr Schroeder, reports of your work have come to me. I'd like to show you more of our glorious Reich. You would marvel at the happiness of our brethren as they join us in a Greater Germany, as we complete the dream of Frederick the Great and Bismarck."

"Mr. Churchill was pleased you kept your agreement and allowed so many British and French to escape the panzers at Dunkirk."

Hitler waived off the comments. "My delegation to the British made it clear we would do what we said we would do, as long as any agreement was upheld. Churchill filled his part of the bargain, so I did mine. Ultimately we would like the British to join with us, so killing them made no sense. Taking those resources back to England and giving me the ability to subdue the French without hindrance, well, I'd like to thank your Prime Minister for allowing me to accomplish that deed. Through my envoys I had made it very plain in our talks with the Englanders that we stand up to our agreements and we take great umbrage when those agreements are not abided or are manipulated."

Schroeder held out an envelope, "This is direct from Sir Winston. I do not know what is inside. I was instructed to wait for a reply or an indication that there would be no reply, and return such to the Prime Minister."

Hitler produced a smile that was in halves benign and a grimace. He handed the envelope, unopened to an aide, who used a small knife to slice it and briefly scanned the contents.

"We will provide you with an answer before you leave. For my part Professor Schroeder I need you to undertake a great mission for me. It could prove decisive and help set the course of Germania and perhaps all of Europe, for a 1,000 years."

"Receiving the crown of Charlemagne has opened my eyes to the possibilities of a united Europe. And events have brought such unity within reach. Bismarck did the work of uniting German peoples and I have completed that work with the addition of our Germanic brethren. I now propose to bring England, France and Germany together into one powerful European union, with a glorious past and an unlimited future. Such a power is necessary to stand against the growing menace of Soviet Russia."

"And how can I help? I am just an academic, a professor of history, and not schooled in these things."

"You Herr Schroeder are perfectly placed to help us. We require a voice of reason in the halls of the Anglo-American alliance. As an American you can help to soothe American concerns and help them to see a United Europe is not a threat but an opportunity for greater business ties, greater efficiencies and a pliable and likely partner. Your connection to Herr Churchill gives us a voice directly to our most fervent detractor. As a German you can do a great service to our nation."

"However my ties to both those nations are tenuous."

"And that's where you can help us the most. The greatest threat to our success is the British Prime Minister. His predecessor understood the opportunities that exist, former King Edward and King George are sympathetic and they themselves hold a significant German heritage. In fact many in your government and the aristocracy see the value and nobility of our plan. No, the great stumbling block must be eliminated. You need to remove Churchill from office. He stands in the way of history."

Schroeder had not been expecting the request.

"In the parliamentary system one man cannot do more than persuade his fellows. And I am not a politician. Removing Churchill from office is far beyond my ability."

Herr Hitler pursed his lips, "Removal from public life can take several forms."

Schroeder blinked hard.

The aide reading the letter spoke, "Mein Fuhrer, this note is a demand from Churchill to stop the air raids with a threat to destroy Germany utterly, should we fail to stop immediately. He is also demanding that we leave French, Belgian and Dutch territory as quickly as possible. He requires these measures to determine our good faith."

"Send a message to Goring and tell him to immediately cease the air raids."

Schroeder and the German aides stood dumbstruck.

"Tell Herr Churchill we will give him his desire. Stop the raids and let us converse about our shared future," said Hitler. "However, we will not relinquish our hard fought gains in France until we are given more sureties that our plan for a political union is accepted. I understand we need to go slowly. The first step is a cessation of hostilities between us. I am hopeful that by including France in our plan, the British will be satisfied with our good intentions. And if necessary we will take on the Communists by ourselves, hopeful that you will join us. It will come to that Herr Professor. This is my pledge and I hope it indicates to you our willingness to act in unison."

"Is that the message you want me to convey?"

"Yes. We will remove ourselves from France and Belgium at the appropriate time. Though I will not rule out serious actions should our offers be declined. However the time is short in the East, as I would like to commit our resources there and have our ethnic brethren join us in subduing the communist threat."

"Any attempt on Churchill will be seen as an act of war, not a surgical strike to eliminate a stumbling block."

"Perhaps, but unless Churchill joins with us we must try to have him removed, and in such a way that no blame falls on Germany."

"That appears to be a singularly difficult task."

"We have a man on the inside and a plan."

"Not me surely. I am no assassin. Nor am I a political operative able to sow dissent. There must be others, better trained, who could do what you request?"

"Of course there are always alternatives, but you are best positioned entirely because you have access and apparently the confidence of the Prime Minister. First try to gather support for the plan especially among the elected officials and the elite. Should that fail we will have our man in London provide you with the necessary means - poison I think is best. You will not be a suspect and I imagine a gun would be very difficult to get near Churchill and damning in the aftermath."

The party went silent for a short time as Schroeder gathered his thoughts. An attendant brought out several trays of sandwiches.

"I would be much better placed to advocate on behalf of the Union plan. Though I would have to give such an approach much thought, as I am not cognisant of who exactly to approach. I do know there are people in the British Foreign Office who are sympathetic to your plan."

"I can have one of my men provide you with several names, people to get started with.," Hitler mused. "Yes, you should do that. Our other options will be reserved until they are needed, and put in place should Churchill undermine our glorious plans."

"There will be significant difficulty in erasing the ill will of the British in the face of the Blitz. Many hundreds have died at your . . . in the destruction of buildings."

"Our Minister of Public Information, Herr Goebbels, will be tasked with that when the British agree with our plan. A bit of contrition, evidence of good works in rebuilding, and the faith of your King and parliament would go a long way to soothe those feelings in the general public."

"Pardon my ignorance Mein Fuhrer, but if we are establishing a 1,000 year Reich, how will succession be managed. Surely there is a king, currently England's George VI in place but what of the Chancellorship or Prime Ministerial office of the civil government administration?"

"Ah, Mr. Schroeder, such things remain to be discussed. Tell Churchill that I propose two bodies acting in concert and the gradual establishment of a transnational parliament. It merely falls to me to establish this new order, to define its borders, pacify its people and set us on the path that leads to our glorious future. Others will shepherd the Reich beyond that, hopefully within the bounds we establish, much like your Americans who still live within the laws established after their revolution more than 150 years ago.

This is our Revolution from the past and the stumbling blocks of history. It is not long since Germany began its path towards unification."

Schroeder reasoned he could let events play out and hope his disappearance would satisfy the Germans, or he could tell Hitler that he was finished as a spy and would have no more access to Churchill.

"I can arrange for you to be delivered by plane to England across the Channel, once the English have cleared you."

Schroeder could see no way out. He had to agree to help but return in the manner that was planned so he could be disappeared, an event that would cover his lack of compliance. However with his safe passage back to England assured by the Germans, they might have trouble believing he was killed during his travels. He knew he had no choice and was prepared to go along with the plan in order to buy some time.

"Thank you but I believe I should simply return in my expected manner. Such treatment would make me look like a collaborator, rather than a Briton who believes in union. Perhaps a message to London that I can be picked up at the port at Biarritz? That I have a message from you to the Prime Minister."

"As you wish Herr Schroeder, sometimes difficult things are required to set the course of history. One man is not more important than the end goal, the salvation of millions, and the creation of a super state, capable of philosophical and technical feats so far unheard. You won't be leaving us until tomorrow morning. Please join me for dinner at my home in the valley. I should like to know more about your own background and attitudes given your unique life story. How did an American become interested in European social history of the upper classes?"

"That would be because my grandfather left Germany due to its socially constricting nature, such that it was in the late 1800s. He was a very capable man who felt trapped by social constrictions of the old guard. I wanted to understand."

"Precisely the same way I have felt. I want a Germany where historical privilege is gone and merit reigns. And I want that in all aspects of society, business, art, sport, philosophy."

Schroeder was intrigued by Herr Hitler, finding him not to be the caricature of German pigheadedness tinged with a touch of madness, as he had been portrayed in England.

The party left the Eagle's Nest. Hitler had invited Schroeder to ride with him but an SS guard shook his head gently reminding Hitler of security protocols.

"Apparently I am wanted by my advisors to conduct some business on the ride. You will excuse me. We can continue our conversation at my home. We will return you to your hotel tonight and you will be escorted to the Swiss border tomorrow morning.

Three staff cars moved down the mountain. Hitler in the middle one with a pair of aides. Schroeder rode in the rear car, joined by Major Kilhofer, while the lead car held a number of armed security men.

The little parade moved down the mountain, winding slowly through the switchbacks, past the sentry station and back to the main road.

The sedate ride back gave Schroeder a few minutes to think. He had no intention of attempting to assassinate Sir Winston. If his extraction from Occupied France went according to plan, and a very uncertain plan it was, he would be in England with both the Germans and the Americans thinking he had been killed leaving Europe. But that also meant that his message from Hitler would not be 'officially' delivered. If Germany had people inside the

British government perhaps they would uncover the truth.

With no sign of trouble and only a few miles from Obersalzberg just north of Berchtesgaden, the small group of cars wound through the hilly countryside.

With a high slope on their left and a deep ravine on their right the staff cars moved slowly down the mountain. Schroeder first noticed it out of the corner of his eye, a large black truck gliding down the hill on the left toward and intersection with the main road. Almost as soon as he had noticed it, the truck appeared to be out of control, speeding up rather than slowing as it approached the road and moving too quickly for its size, gathering momentum as it rolled down the hill. The car with Kilhofer and Schroeder screeched to a halt to avoid a collision. The truck flew through the main road, and plowed into the middle car in their convoy, pushing it off the road and down into a steep ravine. The truck almost went down with it, but remained precariously on top, it's cab tilted sickeningly over the edge.

The two other cars stopped and soon the area was filled with machine gun toting security. Several men from the cars leapt out and headed for the ravine. As they plunged down the steep slope still covered in spots with snow, there was a rapid and muffled sound of gunfire, for perhaps 10 or 15 seconds. Then again spotty reports from shots, and then nothing. Several men reappeared from the ravine and fanned out walking along its top. Then silence, save for the escape of pressured air and gas from the wreck.

Schroeder got out of the staff car and turned toward the ravine.

A hand gripped him firmly on the shoulder impeding his progress. "Herr Schroeder, you might be best to leave, I can't imagine the SS are going to be too civil to any foreign interests right now."

Major Kilhofer was standing beside him.

"But I have done nothing wrong. And certainly running away would make this look like a plot rather than an accident."

Kilhofer gave him a long look, and replied quietly, "It is no accident Herr Schroeder. And for you it is unfortunate that you happen to be in the midst of it. Come with me, it is best we both disappear completely and quickly. Reprisals will begin shortly."

Kilhofer returned to the car and told the driver to join the security men who were searching the ravine. Then he jumped into the driver's seat and motioned Schroeder to get in. They slowly pulled around the accident scene, with  Kilhofer rolling down a window and telling a pair of SS men standing on the side of the road that he would go into town and send emergency workers. They nodded and saluted.

"My inclination is to head north as they will not expect us to drive deeper into the Reich. However, I'd guess it will take them more than an hour to determine we have gone missing. In that time we should be able to get to the Swiss border."

The car moved through town, stopping to report the accident and then moving on south and west towards Switzerland.

"How do you know it was a plot?"

"My dear Schroeder, you really are not a spy. First, there was gunfire at the bottom of a ravine after a traffic accident. There were gunmen already down there. Second, the accident was perfectly executed on only the most important vehicle.  And third it was I who tipped off the truck driver."

"So Hitler is dead?"

"I cannot know that for certain. But the gunfire tells me that anyone who may have survived the tumble down the slope was eliminated where they fell. It is a virtual certainty."

Schroeder gulped. "This presents enormous complications."

"Enormous opportunities I hope," said Kilhofer. "I am hopeful that the war will end and that the insane path we were on, has been avoided. You heard Herr Hitler speak of eliminating the Russian threat. An offensive war with the Russians has little chance of success and seizing their lands would only lead to a perpetual state of war."

They travelled in silence, Schroeder unable to think past the jumble of conflicting notions the events had spurred. The black staff car rolled up to the Swiss border. Kilhofer did the talking.

The Swiss processed all that they were told, insisted that Kilhofer and Schroeder remain under house arrest. They were taken to a nearby hotel and were told to remain in their room while official enquires were made. There was a double guard at their door and another at the entrance to the hotel. Late the next afternoon there was a knock at their door and a uniformed officer immediately entered.

"We have been able to corroborate that something very significant had happened in Obersalzburg," the officer said. He threw a package on the bed. "Here are some civilian clothes for you Herr Major. We will continue our investigation as to the exact nature of the event."

"Are we free to leave?"

"Free? That depends on your definition of 'free'. It is evident that you both cannot stay here. In fact, I have never seen you, nor you me. You will be taken to Geneva quickly and removed into France. At that point you are on your own. We do not wish to be implicated or to invite the wrath of anyone, especially the Nazis. Neutrality has its obligations."

Kilhofer tried to beg his way into staying in Switzerland but the authorities refused. They wanted no traces of their involvement. The two were taken with speed across the mountainous country and told to either cross the border themselves or disappear within 12 hours. If they were still in Switzerland after that, they would be considered to have illegally entered the country.

Schroeder began his escape now realizing his German guaranteed passage was void. His disappearance pointed to him as a conspirator. He was expected by American interests to divert to Portugal once he arrived at Le Puy. But he wanted to find a British contact in that city, and he had to do it secretly. The British plan was to intercept him and take him back to England through Bordeaux. Now he had the burden of being sought by authorities and a fugitive SS officer to deal with, complications he could not avoid.

# Chapter Eleven - Escape from France

Schroeder and Kilhofer slipped into France with the help of the underground. The French Alps were a warren of pathways, streams and unguarded mountains through which an enterprising and determined person could travel and avoid official crossings. From there Schroeder and Kilhofer were taken to Chamonix in the back of a hock cart and then to Annecy and Grenoble. At Grenoble they waited for a change of minders to take them to Valence and to Le Puy where they were to meet up with the American underground and be escorted through the Pyrenees to Portugal. They all agreed this plan was safer than trying to exit through the a western port and the Nazi Atlantic wall.

Schroeder could feel the tension among those he travelled with. The Swiss had looked the other way when he crossed into France a few miles from a main road. Meeting a Frenchman he had explained who Kilhofer was and the grimace from the underground operative, and the flash of fear in his eyes, made him wish he had separated from the SS Major before entering France.

Holed up in a Chamonix hotel basement the nascent French Resistance debated killing the SS man outright, as they felt his story was a set up. Kilhofer accepted their security concerns without complaint but made it plain that he wanted to return to Austria or Germany where he would remain underground until such time as the regime changed.

The news that Hitler was most certainly dead failed to break the ice with the French they encountered.

"All I ask is that you monitor communications and activities, that alone will likely lend credence to our claims."

"Did you see him die?"

"No, as I explained it was an arranged traffic accident and an ambush to ensure the result. I expect several of our resistance fighters in Austria died in the effort."

The French for their part were unhappy escorting a known SS officer through their network and insisted upon blindfolds and frequent changes of course, traveling mostly back roads and during busy times. In eastern Vichy France the local administration held sway but put up with incursions of Italian and German armed groups as long as they caused no trouble. The method of administration in these areas was still under some debate and the Nazis, unexpectedly in control of western Europe, had not entirely decided what to do with the vast territory they had captured.

"Hurry, you cannot stay here. The Germans have descended on the area. It appears they are looking for the both of you."

Having few things the two men were hustled into the back of a truck and left town as quickly as possible, heading for a mountain cabin near Annecy, a regional town to the west.

"You must stay here tonight. The Germans appear quite determined in their search but they likely will not reach small cabins in the woods, at least tonight. I am not supposed to do this, but here is my pistol. Use it only at the greatest need and please return it to me when I pick you up tomorrow morning. We will leave early and hope to out run their search."

Vichy France had been declared only a few days before and the reality of it was still a matter of some conjecture, especially among Italians who coveted parts of the French Alps.

The occupiers resorted to casual violence often as a way to enforce their will and cow the populace but of course that approach stirred up more trouble. The Italians wanted a piece of eastern France and pushed their way into the country but they were not as organized as the Nazis and their sway was local.

The French resistors were only too happy to return Kilhofer to Germany and made it plain that they wanted him out of their jurisdiction fearing reprisals if he was found in the area.

Kilhofer wanted to return to Germany through Bavaria but the high level of German activity looking for the escaped pair made that impossible. The only alternative was to remove him from France along with Schroeder, a prospect that Christoph realized was fraught with difficulty given his plan to evade the Americans and escape back to Britain. He reluctantly decided that Kilhofer's fate was not his responsibility.

Each time they were handed off to the next underground contact there was joy at the prospect of Hitler's death, but curiously all the Frenchmen did was look at each other in disbelief. The signals out of Germany were ragged and there was no official word, but the man hunt in France for the two apparent conspirators was intense.

Still hopeful for regime change Kilhofer felt his place was back with those opposed to the Nazis. His French hosts agreed. But without any indication that things in Germany had changed and with the manhunt still chasing at their heels they decided to try to get out and let events dictate their next moves. Word came through the underground that Schroeder would be met with an American escort at Le Puy for the trip southwest over the Pyrenees and into Portugal and eventually the United States. Kilhofer stuck to the plan and joined him.

Schroeder quietly stuck to his British exit plan but in the swirling confusion Schroeder knew he had to manage this part of the operation perfectly or his disappearance would not be believed. They were moved to an apartment in Puy en Velay, the moderate sized city where the transfer was to take place. Kilhofer admitted to Schroeder that he still wished to return to Germany but was resigned to escape through Portugal.

As they were given a few buns to eat and some tea their underground minder said, "We've made contact with your Americans. You are to go with them tonight."

At the appointed hour Schroeder shouldered his small pack and left with Kilhofer and a guide.

Flitting down deserted streets, Schroeder wondered why they had chosen this conspicuous time to move safe houses. If German searchers were still about they would be particularly vulnerable.

Crossing behind a lit up hotel on the corner of a cul-de-sac and a twisting main road, Schroeder could see one of the soaring volcanic columns particular to Le Puy looming ahead of him. The other was hidden by the buildings on the street and only visible as a silhouette as the road opened up to side streets. These columns were several hundred feet high, with one the home to a small church at the top and the other a large statue of Jesus.

Schroeder realized he had to disappear before he met his American contact. His underground minder told him and Kilhofer to wait as he travelled to the next quiet place before waving him forward, having made sure the areas was secured from on-lookers. They moved one at a time with stealth through the shadowy streets, leap-frogging from one to the next secure location. They managed this mode of movement twice before Schroeder realized it provided his chance to disappear. Any one of these hops could land him among the Americans and make his disappearance more difficult.

Nearing the volcanic column he used its moonlit shadow to disguise his change of course. Kilhofer went first at the minder's all clear signal and disappeared into the darkness. Schroeder waited until he was gone and then turned down a likely side street and stopped in the shadows of a building before concealing himself in an alley. He heard his minder hoot and he hooted back but quickly moved even further away, repeating the hoot when a faint distress call was heard. He moved quickly from the area, and hoped he could meet with his British contact before his conspicuous movements were picked up by locals or a Vichy patrol.

He crouched in the garden of a small house his senses heightened to any sound. There was nothing. He propped himself up against a shed and waited.

Eventually a crease of dawn lit up the eastern sky and he knew he had to find sanctuary where he had agreed to meet his British contact.

He was to go to the Cathedral Notre Dame-du-Puy, located a few hundred yards south of the volcanic pinnacle. There he would blend in with the morning visitors and hopefully be spotted by a British agent.

As the light in the sky grew he moved towards the church, first scouting it out from a distance, then remaining outside its immediate environs, watching the entrance carefully.

Traffic increased. People made their way inside, presumably for Mass, but Schroeder remained on his bench unwilling to be caught up in a service or create any commotion. He sat, hyper aware of the swirl of the morning, taking note that nearby shops were opening. He feared being found by the French underground or the Americans who were likely looking for him. He decided to venture into the church as he felt vulnerable being in the same spot for too long.

As he came to this decision he watched a number of people exit the church, indicating morning mass was complete. He resolved to move across to the church when he felt a hand on his shoulder.

He stiffened and gasped.

A voice quite close to his ear said, "Monsieur, it is a lovely monument."

"It is, but it's my first time seeing it." He turned his head to look at the man accosting him. It was Tommy, Winston's man who had helped him get from Edinburgh to London. He spoke in perfect French. Schroeder visibly relaxed.

"Come, we need to get you out of here. The underground is looking for you and the Americans are frantic."

Tommy escorted him to a nearby car and told him to keep his head down. The car moved off and merged into traffic moving away from the center of town to the east.

"I think we are getting better at this stuff mate. That went very smoothly." He had reverted to his East End accent.

"For you maybe, but I spent a rather worrying night not knowing where I was or who was looking for me."

"Everybody was looking for you. Me included. You're fine now. Mission accomplished, well at least the hard part. Now the French underground and the Americans think you've gone missing. Let's hope they don't think you are a double agent. All we have to do is get you to La Rochelle and back to England."

"I had an escaped SS Major with me. He was going to be evacuated by the Americans. There is reason to believe that Hitler is dead. He was implicated and helped me get out of Austria. The Nazis think I, we, had something to do with it and they are scouring the countryside for us."

Tommy grimaced, "Well that explains a few things. We need to be extra careful."

With the official machinery of Vichy France still being put into place the chief concern was the populace many of whom were anxious to get brownie points from their new masters. Armed Nazis patrolled the roads but as yet no road blocks had been set up. Tommy said he expected that would change shortly.

The Americans waiting for him in the Pyrenees to get him to Portugal had to report he had not arrived, even though Kilhofer was delivered to them. Anderson received a report from Washington, through a low ranking member of the American Embassy in London, explaining that Schroeder had left with a guide to find the contact but they had become separated and Schroeder never arrived for the rendezvous. However an SS Major on the run had been scooped up and was in Portugal awaiting transit back to the States.

Anderson was stopped in his tracks. He had believed that the British were planning to remove Schroeder from France through Biarritz but his contacts in the British government suggested he did not arrive at that extraction point either.

Anderson's time with Schroeder had been playful and he had never feared for him. He did receive confirmation that Schroeder had delivered the American message to members of the underground in Vichy.

Tommy moved Schroeder to a British safe house in the countryside west of Le Puy and quickly moved him to the western port of

La Rochelle, situated halfway up the French western seaboard. The Germans were busy securing those ports closer to Portugal, Spain, England and Ireland, leaving La Rochelle for last. It was a large estuary  with port access to the sea and made for a good place to execute their plan. With everyone looking for traces of him in the south, generally in Biarritz or into the Pyrenees, he had officially been lost to an unknown fate.

The extraction was conducted the same way as his previous exit from France at Dieppe. This time however he and Tommy were simply guided to a beach on a small island just north of La Rochelle and they waited. Within an hour a small boat became visible on the sea and the motorized launch moved into shore quickly.

Tommy gave a signal and was recognised.

"Christoph, let's go quickly and meet that boat."

Hands reached for them as the boat approached the shore, "Come, if getting wet is the worst that happens we will be lucky. I am Lieutenant Alfred Cross, we need to move."

They waded into the surf and jumped into the launch, quickly making their way out into the open ocean. A mile or two off shore a small fishing vessel lay bobbing on the swell. They scrambled aboard and the larger boat moved off, first heading west, out to sea and then swinging north.

A plane cut the air above them.

"A routine patrol. Not sure if they saw our coming aboard."

The plane swung around and circled their position.

"Well, we've excited their interest anyway."

A second plane reached their position and then they noticed two boats converging on them. Their captain ordered the fishing nets raised in hopes that the nets would kill any interest from the patrols.

They moved out to sea, almost directly west.

One of the patrol boats reached them and hailed them to stop. Their captain refused, signalling they were in international waters.

The patrol signalled back that they were in a war zone and fired a shot into their hull. Tommy had been donning the garb of a fisherman and Schroeder was hustled into the hold, currently a quarter full of fish. He climbed in and sunk himself among the catch, keeping his nose above the slimy, wriggling living mass. He could hear the heavy boots of the boarders and tried to keep his heart from racing while practicing holding his breath.

On deck the Germans made to confiscate the vessel and tow it into harbour. As they made good on tying a tow line an explosion was heard on the German patrol boat and then several shots rang out. The tow line was cut and the fishing boat hove to and the engines whined as it moved quickly to full throttle.

Schroeder lifted himself upright and moved to exit the hold.

Tommy peered in and reached out his hand to hoist him back to the deck.

"Not sure who had the worst of it. But I guess it was the Jerries." He grinned lopsidedly and jerked his thumb over his shoulder. Schroeder looked out and saw the German patrol boat smoking some distance off, with significant damage to the foredeck where the single 50 caliber gun was located. There was a body on the deck of the fishing boat which quickly made a distance from the damaged German vessel.

"We gotta move quick and hope they didn't radio for assistance or air cover."

"What about the second boat?"

"They saw what happened but appear to be tracking us. We can probably expect planes in due course."

The minutes ticked by with those on the boat expecting to see evidence of a plane or a squadron coming from the French coast. Eventually three planes did join them but they were British fighters which buzzed around them as they made their way north. Several German planes caught them as they approached the British coast but with the British air cover they did not engage. The fishing boat did come to dock at Penzance, the captain deciding thanks to the air cover he would make for a shorter trip than a journey to Ireland, further from the French shore but leaving them vulnerable for longer. A group of German fighters tracked them and one, managed a strafing run despite the efforts of the British air escort. A few moments of terror and a number of bullet holes in the boat were the only damage inflicted.

* * * * * * * * * *

An aide rapped sharply on the door of the Prime Minister's study at 10 Downing Street. Churchill had made the room his own but was loathe to abandon his apartment at the Admiralty. His aides made it plain that of his several known residences, he was safest at Downing Street, thanks to the bunker built beneath it, and yet they were anxious that he move around so targeting him would be more difficult.

Despite their insistence he often went to the roof to watch the German bombing runs, oblivious to the danger, or perhaps revelling in it. Churchill had been making his own myth for decades and was not about to stop in the face of German bombers who were more interested in factories and docking facilities than they were monuments and masonry which characterised Westminster.

Chartwell was in the process of being mothballed as it was too easy a target for bombers and assassins, and too difficult to secure. So he would decamp on weekends to Chequers Court, a country home outside of London that was gifted to the nation some years before and served as a Prime Ministerial retreat. He also spent time at the homes of other prominent Britons, enough to disguise his travels.

Churchill, on his way to Chequers, thought his aide was going to impart something regarding the journey about to begin. He was wrong.

"We have him sir, he just boarded the fishing boat off the coast of La Rochelle. He is reporting that Hitler may have been assassinated."

Churchill pondered the news and held himself back from communications with the boat. He would have to wait for details.

"Jeremy, please arrange for fighter support for that fishing vessel. Waves of fighters. And instruct our radio men to be particularly vigilant for any unusual signs and communications coming from the Germans."

"Apparently our man had a harrowing journey across France. We were right about Biarritz and Bordeaux as they've been bottled up. The Nazis are near to securing the country. It appears your suggestion that La Rochelle would be last was right."

Schroeder was moved quickly to Oxford where he remained for a fortnight. Notices were sent out as to his disappearance and eventually his flat in Ealing was cleared and his things returned to him via Churchill.

Churchill met with Schroeder at Blenheim Palace, his ancient home.

"This is the first time I've been back here in years," said Churchill looking about. "I thought it best if you were not seen anywhere. I have secured you a professorship at St. Andrew's University north of Edinburgh. I suggest you change your appearance. Perhaps a beard or mustache. That will keep you out of circles, as will the name change. You are now Professor Merrimack, Andrew Merrimack. It will help you to remain of American extraction, given your accent. And first you will be sent to Newcastle for a few days to help you acclimatize to your new name and circumstances."

"That appears to be an end to my academic climb then."

"Oh no, once you've established yourself in Scotland, and provided yourself with a record of sorts, you will be provided with a tenured position at Oxford, Magdalen College, I believe, once all of this is over."

"And the paper on the Victorian nobility?"

"Ah yes that. Well it cannot be published now, can it? Perhaps another short article, something that may have already been in the publisher's hands might pay a bit, but there can be no follow up. We don't want to hint that you are around to finish it. Don't worry I will secure you a publishing contract for the work which can be written under a pseudonym and published after the war, say as a person who had access to your notes. Your death is a sad story really. I have contacts in publishing you know."

Schroeder nodded. He was grateful that his situation was being managed but unhappy that he would have to start over again in the far north.

"I've never been to Scotland. What's it like?"

"Very nice, the Scots are particular and determined. They are British rather than English, always remember that, and they are efficient and industrious. Edinburgh in particular is lovely."

"But I'm not going to Edinburgh."

Churchill laughed, "No you are going to a university town nearby. Think of it as Oxford is to London."

"All this 'service to my country' stuff was just supposed to be a lark. Now things will never be the same. Will my family in the States know I'm alive?"

"First you will be reported as missing. Then we will suggest we believe you are a prisoner of war, and then eventually you can tell them you are alive but must remain distant and communicate with them only in code. The death of your former self will be reported as a boating accident. A sad tale actually. We will work all of that out in the future."

"What about Hitler's death? Are there any indications of it?"

Churchill took a deep breath, audibly pushing it out between his clenched teeth. "It remains a mystery. Certainly there was a flurry of activity reported in the 72 hours after your escapade, though of course we did not know we should be looking until later. Chatter has died down but curiously Hitler has remained sequestered with no public appearances that we can confirm."

"What of Kilhofer?"

"We have nothing from the Americans on that and hesitate to bring it up as it will bring the whole affair into greater scrutiny."

"And you sir, you are a target."

"Your revelation from Hitler is perhaps not a surprise, as my security people keep saying, but I had no idea he thought me the linchpin in British resistance. It is not just me."

"You cannot keep the Nazis guessing forever and when they decide against you, they will attack with redoubled ferocity."

"I will keep them guessing for now. Air raids have slowed almost to a stop and I have already received a communiqué from Berlin asking for a meeting. We have decided to arrange for the appearance of an assassination attempt on me. We would like to keep your façade up as the Germans likely know you are not dead. It might help protect you in the future."

"It might also attract more attention to me should the Germans figure out where I am."

"No, we will cover your tracks and suggest in whispers that you have been tried in secret by a military court."

"I do not like any of this. I simply want a quiet life. I am no spy."

"Maybe not sir, but you are a conduit. We will make it look like you are captured in the failure, without any specifics to be sure."

"How will you stop the Americans from getting this news? And what of future Nazi actions?"

"They have stopped the air raids. You said Hitler had ordered it. Though it might be attributable to a purge after an assassination attempt. Certainly the Nazis are keeping up the façade that Hitler is still in charge, but there are indications of drift in their actions. It is possible that the German High Command simply took charge, either as Hitler recovers from the attempt or in the wake of his death. Hitler was not the only committed Nazi in Germany. As for the Americans, perhaps you are right. Let's hold off on the alleged assassination for now. It can be our ace in the hole."

* * * * * * * * * *

Schroeder, now known as Andrew Merrimack took up his position at St. Andrews. He maintained a low profile and the university chancellor kept him at arm's length, knowing that his tenure had been engineered, and given the understanding that this new professor should melt into the background at the university.

Merrimack deliberately moved his specialty from social mores of Victorian Britain to the political history of wars of succession from the time of the Plantagenet Edwards in 1272 through the establishment of the English House of Hanover with the four King George's ending in 1820. This 550 year swath of English history took the country from a forgotten outpost to the verge of Empire. The array of royal marriages were instrumental in cementing English power and influence during this period. However it was the brute strength of arms that kept it together. It was an almost constant warfare in which nobody seemed surprised by the inability of victories to put an end to the fighting or cement any lasting peace. Scotland was only too aware of this strain of history and Merrimack found he had to proceed gently among those still aggrieved by English actions which occurred hundreds of years before.

Through the summer months air raids from Germany were sporadic and usually aimed at military installations. Merrimack could not help but wonder if negotiations on the Northern Kingdom plan were moving forward. He tried to put it out of his mind. As the air raids ended Merrimack thought that Churchill had been able to keep the Northern Kingdom plan afloat and that the Germans had abandoned their pressure, and unleashed their efforts against the Russians. Such a change in plan, such an abrupt about face, suggested that Hitler was either mad or dead, and someone else had taken command.

As time passed Schroeder realized either Hitler had survived or the German's had planted an imposter into his place and continued the march towards a Greater Germany. Of course Hitler could never have risen to power if there were not a large number of sympathetic Germans in and out of the military.

True to Schroeder's guess, the terror bombing tactic simply back-fired on the Nazis, with the British and Churchill entirely determined to withstand the Nazis and remain clear in their belief that the Nazi approach to the world was entirely wrong.

It was a miserable Christmas of 1941 but Merrimack received a letter from the United States. His family had been told of his new identity and they wrote an open ended letter to him skirting all the issues of secrecy both real and imagined. Merrimack wrote back in the same guarded vein but included a promise to continue correspondence and hopefully return to the US for an extended visit upon completion of the hostilities.

The Germans played one final card in the days before the Nazi invasion of Russia, and asked Churchill for a meeting regarding the Northern Alliance.

"Professor Merrimack?" A short, well dressed man had tapped on his office door and stuck his head in.

"Yes, what can I do for you?"

The man took a deep breath, "Our mutual friend Winston would like a word with you."

Merrimack started. His mouth went dry. He had not heard anything from Winston or anyone associated with his previous activities for several months. He had however been convinced that he saw Tommy or one of the other British agents wander about campus, but he could never be sure.

"Where? How?"

Something beat within him, not so much the desire to serve, but to help Winston and to know what his part in all of this was going to be. There was a cross cut desire to be done with everything and never call it to mind.

"A short meeting at a house outside of town. A few hours only. Winston is touring some naval facilities nearby and could meet with you tomorrow. You would only be gone from here for a few evening hours."

And so Merrimack jumped into a cab that awaited him the next night after supper and was driven for less than an hour west to a country home.

"Ah, Professor Sch- Merrimack, so nice to see you."

"And you Mr. Prime Minister."

"I'll forgo the niceties now, but will return to them once we finish our pressing business," Churchill smiled around his cigar. He let out a few quick puffs as he thought how to frame his request. He took a sip of scotch and offered some to Merrimack.

"Professor, the Nazi's have requested that I attend a meeting with Herr Hitler on a proposal for a new Northern Alliance. They are fearful of the Russians and seek our help. They appear desperate. They have abandoned the plan for a joint Kingdom and have ratcheted it down to an alliance. Given their aggression against the Russians we cannot be party to this. But if playing along will stop or end the war in the west, then I have to agree. I would like unconditional surrender but if they simply stop fighting and declare peace we will have to take notice."

"They want you dead sir, they fear you as the main obstacle to their plans."

"I know it, I should not survive such a meeting, though I am very interested in finding if Hitler is still alive. He is supposed to attend."

"He won't. He could never leave Germany. Even if he is still alive."

"Given that they requested the meeting, it appears they are desperate. I'm guessing that they require the Luftwaffe resources elsewhere and want to conclude their operations against us."

"So why not wait them out?"

"Perhaps, but how many more will die by waiting. There is no indication of when they will stop and it is only a guess on my part that they will. I could be wrong you know. The probability of that is small but parsing out the details is a mug's game.

"So I think we have to send a delegate with considerable power to negotiate. I am thinking of one of the War Cabinet members. In addition, I'd like you to go, disguised as you are now, as you are perhaps the only person who has seen Hitler and can vouch for his authenticity."

Merrimack asked for the details of the meeting and Churchill provided them. A small contingent from both sides, would meet for one day in Geneva, Switzerland, a neutral nation, the meeting sanctioned by the Swiss who would provide the bulk of security. Safe passage was assured for an airplane to make the trip.

"But Hitler will not attend. And he is most likely dead."

"It is our opportunity to determine that face to face. You would attend as a translator under yet another assumed name. I expect they know you are alive, but we don't want to give them a road map of your whereabouts do we?"

"They offered me safe passage back to England and I refused. They must have guessed something was up. And who knows where Major Kilhofer stands in any of this."

"I expect they have spent some resources trying to find you and him. Have you had any contact?"

"No sir. I would have informed you of any contact. I have been living a quiet life for some months now and am only now beginning to feel free of my former situation."

"I should very much like it if you would attend. When they find out that I will not attend, I expect they will make excuses for Hitler but with you there as a translator perhaps we can cut through and find the truth of Hitler's circumstances. Any delay in their plans or uncertainty of our part is beneficial."

"Hitler or his delegates will appeal to our mutual fear of the communists. I certainly do not expect to see him. You cannot go, and in fact should make it plain that you are delegating a high level surrogate. Any deception will not be met happily, and as one of the attendees, I should not like to face it."

# Chapter Twelve - December 1941

And so the British contingent flew in a single plane from Biggin Field south of London to Geneva Switzerland. Churchill had designated an inner member of his former shadow intelligence group but remained out of sight in London at No. 10 Downing Street the entire day.

In addition to the pilots, seven men took the trip including four security agents. Churchill's delegate, an aide to be an extra set of eyes and handle any paperwork necessary, and Merrimack who was designated as a translator.

The Germans were allowed the same number. A call came in from outside the hotel to bring the British to the meeting.

The British refused, saying the hotel was not up to standards and requested that the meeting be moved to a second hotel across town. They suspected that the Germans had made nefarious arrangements at the first locale and insisted upon the change.

The Germans reluctantly agreed and the British were taken by standard taxis to the meeting spot. The second floor of the hotel housed a moderate sized ball room, on this day fitted out with two rows of tables and chairs facing each other. Each side had an exit to the room behind them. The Swiss insisted they all be unarmed and took great pains to insure it.

The two delegations met. They took a break and met again.

Getting a tea, a German in a suit sidled up to Merrimack. "Just pour a touch of this in Churchill's tea."

Merrimack pursed his lips and slid the small bottle into his palm. He considered the implications of any reaction. If he spoke out the meeting would fail into threats and accusations. If he did nothing, the Germans would think he was biding his time.

"We require a decision today," said the lead German negotiator. "Let us adjourn and reconvene in three hours."

The British group left the ball room. They decided to leave Geneva and arranged for a hotel porter to deliver a note at the end of the three hour wait saying they could not agree to an alliance.

"They may try to shoot our plane down."

"So we need more time. Ask the porter to wait until the Germans wonder where we are, before delivering the note."

"That might buy us 15 minutes."

"And that's all we might need."

"It's a three hour flight back to England, buy us that extra time."

The British personnel moved off quickly, leaving in ones and twos and convening at the airfield. As he left Merrimack sent a note saying the British needed a bit more time as one of their party had become unwell.

A knock on the door and Merrimack opened it to a smiling Franz Kilhofer. He was dressed as a hotel porter.

"Major?"

"Hitler is dead. There is an imposter in place. They are desperate for peace in the west. My contacts say the invasion of Russia is in peril as they have made less progress than they hoped and the weather is a larger enemy than the Bolsheviks."

Kilhofer handed Merrimack a note, "This is information on how to contact the German underground - it is highly sensitive. Read it and destroy the paper. Kilhofer left, passing two men in the hallway as he wandered towards the stairs. The men came to the British suite.

"We would like an idea of where our talks are going before agreeing to extend the meeting time, again."

Merrimack said there was no need for a meeting, that they were waiting on the health of their chief negotiator.

The second German was the man who passed the vial of poison. He gave Merrimack a long look and the Professor returned a knowing glance, which appeared to satisfy the Nazi.

He spoke up to his colleague, "Come, a few more hours might make a big difference."

"As a conciliation and show of good faith we will cease any further bombing campaigns in the British Isles."

"A laudable start, but we had been told that that arrangement had already been made several months ago. And while they have been scaled back dramatically, they have not ceased entirely."

"The Luftwaffe has their own agenda."

"Herr Hitler cannot control his own generals?"

The German's expression was sour and he left. Merrimack and the last remaining security man made ready to leave.

They headed for a utility stair that British security had already determined was the quickest way to the street. It was the same exit that Kilhofer had chosen. They made their way as quickly as they could down and exited the building. Merrimack's head was reeling, as he looked for a cab and a clean escape.

Merrimack made to hail a taxi but the security men stayed his hand.

"Not yet, sir. We need to be further from the hotel to be sure."

They turned a corner and a taxi was waiting with Kilhofer standing beside it.

"You British are a bit too predictable. But I can help you get to the airfield. The Germans cannot stay in Geneva long, nor can they operate as they might on their own soil. Get moving  and you should be clear.

On the drive Kilhofer told Merrimack that Hitler was most certainly dead in the engineered hit in Obersalzburg but he was still unable to confirm it, though every other indication was that Hitler had been replaced by a lookalike.

"Unfortunately our witnesses, the men at the bottom of the ravine, were all chased down and killed in the firefight. German high command has taken over the war with the Nazi faction purging the career officers and following the course they had anticipated from Hitler. However, Hitler's approach of creating internal division, fomenting dissent and forcing the hand of targeted governments to bend to the will of their ethnic German citizens, has been abandoned now that there are no more ethnic Germans outside the Reich. This is evident in the invasion of the Ukraine. The Ukrainians would have embraced the Nazis as liberators. They hate Stalin. But the German High Command treated the Ukrainians as aliens to be exterminated."

"And what of the German invasion of Russia?"

"Yes, and the Russians seek your aid or at least to necessary materials to battle the invasion."

"You seem almost too well informed."

"Perhaps, but there is a contingent of honourable Germans who wish to see Hitler and the Nazis removed from power. There is a split between those who oppose Hitler entirely and those who believe the German unification is laudable and its completion a natural end to hostilities."

"What about German speaking Switzerland?"

"Another story. We are in the safest part of Switzerland, the ethnic French section, but there are still plenty of Swiss who sympathize with the Nazis or wish to curry their favor. We are not safe."

The car swung onto the airfield's tarmac. The last two British bundled aboard the aircraft and it immediately moved off even as the hatch was closing.

A turn over Lake Geneva and a flight path along the former border regions between France and Germany was believed to be their best route back to England.

The pilots monitored several known German frequencies to get an idea if they were being pursued. The silence on the radio was comforting at first but became unbearable as there was so little chatter it seemed unnatural.

Two hours later Cologne was visible in the distance to the east as the plane swung to the northwest. If there was going to be an intercept, it was likely going to be soon.

The planed droned on.

The radio chattered a notice that they would be met with an escort from England as they crossed the Channel. The next 20 minutes were tense with everyone aboard watching, listening and hoping they would be left alone.

A three plane contingent came toward them from the west, but passed behind them. Another plane flew off to their north east.

Schroeder - Merrimack did not breath in relief of the tension until he had stepped from the plane to the solid ground of the Kent countryside. And still it was another touch of relief when he returned to his flat in St. Andrew's.

# Chapter Thirteen - February 1945

Just as the new term began at the University, Professor Merrimack received a visitor in his office at St. Andrews. He had ceased to worry about bumps in the night as his cover appeared to hold.

"I was in the neighbourhood and thought I'd drop around, Professor Schroed . . . er, Merrimack."

Merrimack had looked up when the door opened and could not speak.

It was Churchill himself.

"I am embroiled in a conundrum sir," said Churchill. "I promised anonymity and a quiet life to one who's service warranted it, but I must beg a favour."

Merrimack said nothing but his head dropped to his chest. Churchill continued.

"The Nazis want to discuss peace terms and the Americans think we should at least listen to them, though we are all still strongly in favour of unconditional surrender. There is the pesky problem of the Russians gaining ground each day."

"So talk to them."

"We have decided to do that. The German High Command has requested an envoy. We will not commit to a truce, but if we can suggest to the Germans that their resistance to us should dissolve and they should direct their resources to the east it will help the peace. The Russians appear quite determined to advance west of Berlin, once they have completed their capture of the capital."

"I'd really rather not Sir Winston. Frankly I fear being recognized and I do not have the requisite background for such sensitive talks."

"If you don't we might be missing a great opportunity to end this war early and save countless lives. The Germans are deeply afraid of the Russians, doubly so as they know what horrors they visited upon them as they blitzed the Eastern Front."

Merrimack dropped his head to his chest and closed his eyes.

"It's the power of coercion that I really detest, Prime Minister. As if those future deaths will be on my hands should I fail to jump into the breach."

"As you wish."

Three days later Merrimack was on a submarine in the Baltic. He was being taken to a rendezvous at the mouth of the Oder near the city of Stettin. He met with German General Felix Steiner, Commander of the Army of the Vistula.

"Herr General, greetings."

"Herr, um, Professor Merrimack I have agreed to conduct your visit under a white flag of truce. I will say to you that our cause is lost, the Russians outnumber us and will overrun Germany without something to stop their advance."

"As you know I come at the sanction of Sir Winston Churchill, regarding an idea of mutual benefit."

"Well do sit down, sir. Let's hear your idea."

"We have asked the Soviets to slow their advance. They have refused. We fear the Soviets will not relinquish their gains." Steiner looked pensive and thoughtful as if the idea was new to him. "So we propose a realignment of hostilities to counter that threat."

"Between us we could crush the communist threat."

"At this time we are merely proposing that Germany take control of its eastern frontier and direct all of its resources to the Russian front. Essentially give up belligerent action in the west. The German Empire would be reorganized in the aftermath of hostilities, in full awareness of the mistakes of Versailles."

Steiner trembled. There was no mention of exile. No mention of the new government. All he had to do was coalesce his forces on the Eastern Front. Battle fronts in the south and the west would be ended and those forces moved to confront the Russians.

"Yes. We will do it. We will proceed immediately."

"As you wish. I will communicate your intentions to the Prime Minister and he to the Americans. We will be in further contact. Remember this is not a formal arrangement. We do not wish to raise Russian concerns."

Merrimack returned to Britain and briefed Churchill on the meeting. Churchill thanked him for his service and sent him back to St. Andrews.

"I think it best that your resume your former alias. After the war is concluded you can do what you like, but for now, let's keep the status quo a while longer."

Schroder nodded, glad to be done. As he left, a Churchill aide gave his boss a deep look.

"Schroeder has played his part well. The Germans are fully expecting our help and now they will slow the Russians while we push the Americans more quickly to the east, especially as German opposition will disintegrate."

"Not even history will be privy to our little ploy."

"But Schroeder?"

"Schroeder does not exist anymore in the minds of the Americans. And Merrimack will never say. He fears being drawn in deeper."

# Chapter Fourteen - January 1965

And the years passed. The war ended and Merrimack started a family. He took a chair at Oxford and his war time efforts faded from his every day, especially as few people knew about them.

Nature had helped with his disguise. A receding hairline and a bit of premature aging of his face helped him to remain unrecognised at Magdalen College even though he ran into former colleagues from West London on occasion. A scruff of a Van Dyke style beard also helped complete the image of a professor that was older than his years.

Invited to the funeral of his friend Winston Churchill he decided to shave off his beard so he would not be recognized by his current colleagues.

Two days after the funeral he had succeeded in growing the beginnings of his beard back, but he remained on administrative leave with the Oxford deans looking the other way at the curious circumstance. The department head had instructions from Whitehall.

A few months later an American visitor came looking for him in Oxford.

"Just tell him I would like to speak to him about a paper he wrote on Victorian social conventions."

"I will leave the message."

Upon receiving it, Schroeder - Merrimack was unsure if he should be concerned. Part of him wanted the cloak and dagger to go away and now it was almost 20 years since the war and even more since his part in it ended.

He mentioned the contact to his own Foreign Office contact who he had not spoken to in some time.

"It's up to you now. We would prefer to keep this stuff secret but there is always the possibility you will be found out. You can deny it of course. Or fess up with the Americans.

\* \* \* \* \* \* \* \* \* \*

"You have something?"

"Yes and it's a doosy. A scoot through some documents, and a picture emerges where Schroeder, is essentially an unwilling spy, and he is able to substantially alter the course of the war. In fact, it appears his efforts were instrumental in why the German bombing campaign during the Blitz ended as abruptly as it did. And there was no land invasion. According to our intel, Churchill gave Hitler the ancient crown of the Holy Roman Emperor, that Queen Victoria had squirreled away, in order to secure the Evacuation at Dunkirk. Schroeder was the go-between. And, the British, at the highest levels, were playing footsie with the Nazis. Several high ranking Brits wanted to join with the Germans. Churchill used those negotiations to keep the phony war going and buy time to build planes and increase munitions production. And, they dribbled out just enough to us to get us to commit to help them. And, Schroeder's intel through his American contact, certainly tilted Roosevelt to help the British."

"Any more 'ands'?"

"Does there need to be more?"

"Interesting. This guy appears to be a central figure in World War II and nobody knows it. He is the linchpin in why the Germans allowed Dunkirk to play out the way it did, why they delayed bombing Britain, why the Nazis were so inept in their invasion of Russia, and why they abandoned the western front in the late stages of the war."

"The Brits certainly think so. You don't get an Earldom for nothing. It appears the peerage is Winston's final salute to this effort."

"It all squares with what actually happened and explains how the Brits managed to dodge the Nazis at Dunkirk. Papers have been written about the Nazi failure to capitalize on the fate of the British and French troops who were evacuated. And they all missed this salient fact - it was engineered."

"We must have known about some of this?"

"Some, I think. But how much and exactly what? We knew that Edward VIII was virtually a Nazi but we thought it stopped at that. Hitler was quoted after Edward's visit with him, as saying Wallis Simpson would have made a good queen. Perhaps that comment held more meaning than we previously thought. In any case, the Brits moved Edward to Governor General of Bahamas to keep him out of things, now we know why."

"Makes me wonder what else we don't know."

"Ah, you mean unknown, unknowns?"

"Should we confront this Schroeder?"

"I'm not sure there is any value in it. However, knowing more about that time might come in handy at some point. Whatever became of the crown?"

"I'd never heard of it. I always understood that the crown of Austria was the Holy Roman crown. Perhaps we should ask Schroeder?"

"Churchill obviously didn't value it. And Hitler never acknowledged that he had it. You might almost have expected him to crown himself Emperor, like Napoleon did."

"Probably the reason he didn't. Still, not finding it suggests there are Nazi treasures that we still haven't found."

"I should be shocked that we came that close to Britain siding with the Germans in 1941."

"What a different world it might be if that had happened."

"It apparently would not have taken much to sway the course of history."

"War, my friend is never over. It simply changes into something else. The conflict is always there stewing in the background, just waiting for a bit of heat to bubble up the past."

* * * * * * * * * *

Andrew Merrimack skipped up the step and opened his front door. Cynthia appeared in the hallway, attracted by the rattle of the door opening.

"Well Andrew you are home. You missed the funeral of Churchill. It was broadcast on the telly all day."

"Aye, I saw some of it in the city. I had an engagement there today."

"What an odd day to have scheduled that, London must have been virtually impassible."

Merrimack removed his overcoat, and rubbed his hands together to gain circulation and warm them up.

"It is mighty cold out there. Be thankful you have managed to avoid it."

"Avoid it? How do you think we get dinner on the table every day. I was out in it this morning."

"Sorry love, I just know that I would avoid going out unless absolutely necessary."

She laughed. "Especially without your facial hair. You know, I'm not sure if I like you more with or without the beard. I'm so used to it."

"I'm thinking of growing it back. It was a whim to shave it off, but shaving every single day is more than I anticipated. I probably should have waited until the warmer weather. If you are ambivalent then perhaps I'll go back."

* * * * * * * * *

A few months later when the Queen announced the civil lists for the year, Cynthia Merrimack received the shock of her life. A knock came to the door and she bustled to answer.

"Mrs. Merrimack is your husband Andrew at home? I am from the Daily Mail."

"No. He isn't here, he's at his office at Magdelen."

"Actually he isn't there, they said he was here."

Cynthia dismissed the news reporter and the telephone rang.

"Hello darling, everything alright?"

"Yes, but I just had a reporter here looking for you. Did the dean finally succumb?"

"No, but there is a bit of news that I think you need to hear. Please come and meet me at the Eagle and Child as fast as you can. Nothing to worry about but I'd rather not say over the telly.

Take a taxi."

"A taxi? Such an extravagance," she thought. Cynthia Merrimack made her way into the city and saw her husband was already there waiting for her in a small alcove near the back of the pub.

"So what's all the cloak and dagger?"

Andrew laughed out loud, as he had never laughed before, the wash of news and Cynthia's inadvertent jest breaking the dam. Cynthia had never seen him this way. He stopped and then laughed again, tears beginning to form at the corners of his eyes due to his unbridled joy. She looked at him as if he were mad.

"Andrew?"

"The civil role came out today."

"Yes, okay."

"I've been made an Earl."

Cynthia was silent. She demurely moistened her lips.

"The Earl of Osbourne. I did receive some advance notice, but I must say, I was unsure if it was real and that it would come to pass, so I said nothing."

Cynthia blinked, still unable to fully comprehend the gravity of Andrew's claim.

"You will of course be the Countess of Osbourne, or maybe the Duchess. No that's probably for Dukes. I do not know any details of the investiture or if the title remains with my heirs. Apparently with the title there is an apartment at Osbourne House on the Isle of Wight, if we so choose. Maybe we could retire there at the appropriate time?"

Cynthia merely stared at him, the look of shock slowly changing into one of concern for her husband's mental health.

Andrew laughed, partly in delight and partly at the sight of Cynthia's complete shock.

"I assure you it's all completely legitimate. Winston, Sir Winston, hinted at something like this, years ago, but I had heard nothing of it, until a letter arrived at my office a few days after his death. It was from him, to be mailed to me at that time. It's a good thing you weren't watching the funeral on television too closely as I was there, invited by The Queen herself."

Cynthia cleared her throat soundlessly and moved her lips but no sound resulted.

"Without going into much detail it stems from some services I performed for Sir Winston during the war. You may recall I was unable to serve in the military due to my background as an American of German descent. That background provided me with other opportunities, however. And now I have to decide how to weather this. My colleagues will get wind of it if the newspaper reporters have. I'm afraid our lives will be different. I hope that is not too upsetting."

Cynthia still sat her eyes glazed as if she had so many questions she did not know where to start.

"Whatever shall I wear?"

"A good question. But first we have been summoned to Windsor Castle."

"When?"

"Now actually. I have called for a cab."

# From 'The Cup'

## © F. Bradley Reaume

By F. Bradley Reaume

Castian resolved to attempt to speak with the natives. He took his entire party of armed men, leaving only a few camp attendants to guard their things. The men were all on horseback with their rifles visible as a show of strength. They made for the native camp taking care to approach it from the east so as not to surprise the natives, nor be surprised themselves.

Cantering into the open about a half mile from the natives, he had his men sing a popular song to insure they were spotted from a distance and they approached at a trot, slowing down to give the natives time to ready for their arrival and so they could see how their arrival might be taken.

Two natives quickly mounted their horses and slung rifles over their shoulders, and trotted out to meet the railway group.

The lead native spread his arms out at his waist with his palms open indicating a peaceful approach.

Castian held up his own right hand palm open in an answering greeting and to halt his large group of men. He moved his horse forward and asked the two men on either side of him to approach the natives with him.

Castian was agitated. He did not know what to expect.

"Hello. I am from the Central Pacific Railway. We are wondering what you are doing near our railway line?"

The native narrowed his eyes and cocked his head to the side as if to try to hear better. Castian repeated his question.

The native arched his back to sit tall on his horse. He spoke in a clear and unmistakeable tone. The language was unknown but the tone forthright. He pursed his lips and stared right at Castian. Seeing the railway men look uncomprehendingly he again spread his arms wide but low with his palms out. Then, turned the palms down and patted the air, unmistakeably indicating the natives were intending to camp in this place for some time.

Castian was unsure what to do. He wanted to impress upon the natives that there would be significant repercussions should they interfere with the railway. However he could not communicate such a detailed and obtuse idea.

"Stay away from our railway line and we will have no difficulty with you." He knew it was futile to speak a language they did not understand but he felt better having tried.

The natives looked at each other to see if either of them understood the white man.

Sensing his point was not entirely understood Castian held a single finger in the air asking the natives to hold and wait, vacillating between pointing up and fanning all his fingers with his palm down. He had three of his men on horseback walk in a line and instructed the first in line to throw a handful of dirt into the air while making a whistling sound.

As this was being arranged a few other native warriors had moved from the camp to stand a few yards behind the two natives to whom Castian was 'talking'.

The railway men laughed as they got into position. The natives laughed when they saw the result. But they nodded that they understood.

Castian pointed to the natives and then the train of men and shook his head and waved his hands palms down across each other trying to indicate the natives should have nothing to do with the train.

The natives nodded vigorously. Then one put his hands up and made like he was shooting an arrow down towards the ground. He then held both his hands to his mouth and made chewing motions and licked his lips with a grin.

Castian nodded. He then pointed to the natives and with both hands made sweeping motions to the north away from where the track lay to the south.

The smile slipped from the native's face. He patted the air with his palms face down. The natives were planning on staying. The hunting was good in this place. Castian had been instructed to remove the threat. And even though this group did not seem threatening, he believed he could not leave it in place. He repeated his pointing to the natives followed by emphatic waves to the north.

The native shook his head and pointed to the ground. Sensing his position was not what the white men wanted to hear, he then pointed at his own chest and waved with both hands to the south west. That direction would take the native band right over the rail line somewhere west of Great Salt Lake.

Unsure what to do, Castian figured he could remain and monitor the band for a few days, returning if they did not move off and demanding that they move away immediately.

He nodded and indicated to his group that they withdraw to the south. Once away from the native camp, still under the watch of the natives, they changed course and moved to the west. Castian wanted to explore that territory and look for any signs of the missing scout.

The men picked their way through a forested area generally following a creek which flowed to the south and east. Leaving the creek valley the group moved to the west. If the scout had become disoriented he would have used his compass or the sun to make his way south to  intersect with the railroad and make his way back to camp.

Finding no sign of him the group moved to the north. A rustle in the trees suggested they were being followed, but Castian figured it was only a single warrior who tracked their movements and was unconcerned. He would have arranged the same thing had their positions been reversed.

Castian was on the verge of sending most of his troop back to camp when the forward elements gave a whoop. He trotted forward and saw a body tied to a tree, bloody and pierced with many arrows. Only the clothing made it unmistakably one of his party.

Castian was stunned. The natives had seemed peaceful and while determined to plot their own course they did not appear threatening. This suggested otherwise.

He took a deep breath. To buy time he instructed that the body be taken down, slung over a pack horse and taken back to camp. His men assumed they would all go.

"We cannot let this stand. And we cannot wait. They have been tracking us and may attack in the dark of night."

Mulling the situation over in his mind and constantly returning to his instructions to remove any threat, Castian resolved to immediately attack the native camp. He decided his own camp was not particularly defensible and feared an attack on the native's terms.

The men removed any excess baggage from their horses. They would return to retrieve it should they be able. They split into two groups, and decided to approach the camp from the high ground behind it while feinting an approach from the lower ground to the east.

Moving quickly into position they attacked. The natives were waiting, likely tipped off by their scout that the railway men were returning. The native's secondary camp was in an uproar with teepees being taken down and people moving off to the northwest in an attempt to get into a forested area where they would be less vulnerable from an attack.

Castian sent out a whistle from high on the hill. The force of 20 armed men began to charge the camp from the east. As soon as they were engaged Castian called on his group of 60 men to charge down the hill and through the camp. The natives were waiting.

Halfway down the hill a shot rang out and Castian's horse fell. He was pitched forward and landed with the downward slope cushioning  much of his fall. He rolled down the hill clutching his rifle. The horsemen swept into the camp and shot as many natives as they could at close range. Having guns used against them, the railway men showed no mercy nor any inclination to choose their targets. Castian himself was still on the lower part of the rise carefully taking aim and squeezing off shot after shot. One of the attackers went down. Two horses reared and fell. Arrows found their mark and several attackers were unhorsed. The men from the east continued their charge into the camp and did much the same on a smaller scale.

As the battle was fought there was a steady stream of natives leaving the secondary camp and moving away west.

Soon the resistance faltered. Natives had taken all their shots and had moved off toward the women and children taking horses where they could.

Fearing the natives would reach the other camp and rearm, Castian waved his men in pursuit. He searched out a horse for himself and followed.

The former military men had swords which they unsheathed as they chased after the natives who were mostly running away on foot. Riding hard, the men swept their swords across the backs and necks of those they pursued, dropping them as they ran. Not knowing the men from the women they continued the slaughter in pursuit of any native save the very smallest.

It dawned on Castian that he had best leave no one to speak of the massacre lest other natives revolt and cause far more damage to the tracks than anyone had thought possible.


**'The Cup' is the story of the settling of the frontier West as told through the eyes of former Union soldier Galahad Lake, shopkeepers Gwen and Lance Hopkins, Irish immigrant and newspaper man Percy O'Hagan and a slippery and dissatisfied Morton Castian.**

An excerpt from

# 'A Picture of Distance'

© F. Bradley Reaume

Chas looked at himself in the mirror on his way out the door. Not quite the same 21-year old he had been 40 years before. As he continued his gaze he realized that exactly 40 years ago he had been struggling trying to salvage the engine of a Spitfire that had been hit by anti-aircraft fire during the D-Day invasion.

Walking the beaches now 40 years later lost in his thoughts for the last few days, Chas had enjoyed the time with old mates and his brother Bill. He kept straying to thoughts of Ver Sur Mer and his friend, the pilot Gordon McAuley.

He had written many months ago to The Caen War Memorial to get information on the museum for his trip and inquiring after the final resting place of Bill's friend Frank Edwards and his own wartime acquaintance Simon MacDonald. The museum put him in touch with a Jacques Gaspareau, a member of the French resistance during the war and a local historian.

Mon. Gaspareau wrote back saying that he did indeed know the spot where Lieutenant MacDonald was buried as he had been on a patrol that day in 1944 with his Resistance fighters when he came upon the body of MacDonald. He said the resistance often came across Allied soldiers and secretly buried their bodies to keep them out of the hands of the Nazis who were known to take out their frustrations on the corpses or otherwise denigrate their service.

Mon. Gaspareau said he would be happy to escort Chas to the site and show him around the area.

Chas remembered the events that led to Simon MacDonald's death. He had known Simon as a fellow mechanic. They had become friends as Simon was from the small town of Streetsville, just west of Toronto.

Only a few days after the D-Day landings, with the mechanics busy keeping the landing forces mobile, there had been a late afternoon call from Division for a mechanic to go to the recently seized bridge head outside of Reviers.

Chas was head deep in an engine just as the message arrived. Simon was just making the last few turns with his wrench to finish up the job on his vehicle. He volunteered.

Chas only heard of the events of that day from some of the other boys he had contact with. Simon never returned. When Simon arrived the Germans were apparently in retreat and many Allied tanks and personal were across the river. So Simon ran across the bridge without too much concern to reach a tank that had stalled and partly blocked the bridge egress.

According to those who witnessed it, a squadron of German fighters swooped down on the bridge at that moment and strafed the column trying to squeeze around the stalled tank.

Simon was hit multiple times and knocked off the bridge and into the river. In the chaos of the battle, and not really knowing that Simon was officially there, he was overlooked until several days later when he did not return to the motor pool.

Inquiries provided the story and likely end of Simon MacDonald. His body was not officially found until the burial spot was disclosed after the war. French partisans, including Mon. Gaspareau, found him down river and buried him in a quiet place without much ceremony.

After the war they provided his dog tags to officials who were able to match him up with their records and officially record his burial place. Normandy is dotted with these types of graves, usually unobtrusive, peaceful and enough out of the normal ebb and flow of daily life to be almost forgotten.

Chas was pleased that his inquiries were able to produce MacDonald's final resting place and a guide to help him find it.

Chas called Mon. Gaspareau. Thanks to the Frenchman's very European ability to speak more than one language they were able to quickly agree to a time and place to meet. Chas gave his full name to Gaspareau and began to spell it but Gaspareau stopped him.

"No, no Charles. Stuart is a well-known name around here," said Gaspareau.

Chas expressed surprise. "Oh, well, then I needn't spell it for you. I'll be with my wife. How will I know you on the platform?"

"Do not worry monsieur I will know you – what tourists we get in Ver Sur Mer usually come by car. You will be well known to me on the train platform. I can spot a tourist anywhere," he laughed.

As he hung up Chas smiled at the thought that Mon Gaspareau could see through his attempt to be more restrained than the average tourist.

"It's the running shoes, dear," said Anne, who had been eyeing him eyeing himself. "They give you away, that and the Toronto Maple Leaf jacket you've been wearing. Honestly, even with a few more cameras around your neck, a tour book in your hand and a map in the other you couldn't possibly look more like a tourist."

"At least they don't mistake us for Americans," he said.

"But they do. And if they don't it's because of the jacket dear, not because you don't look the part."

They ambled out of their hotel room in Caen and made their way to the train station where they boarded the train for Ver Sur Mer. Securing their tickets they settled in for a 30 minute ride. Stopping at a number of village cross roads the train never worked up much speed. Soon it was slowing again as they reached their destination. A few of the passengers began to gather their things to disembark. Most appeared to be going on to Bayeux or Cherbourg. Chas and Anne would return to Caen that evening.

The train pulled into the station and it was immediately obvious there was a major ruckus occurring on the platform. It was raucous and crowded. And what first appeared to be some sort of trouble, soon looked more like a huge crowd awaiting a movie star or something.

"There must be a movie star or singer or some celebrity on this train. Listen there's even a band out there."

"Perhaps if we moved up the train we'll get clear of all the commotion. I don't even know what Mon. Gaspareau looks like. I bet he was counting on a quiet day on which to find us."

So the two Canadians moved through a few cars trying to clear the crowds. Chas saw a young man trying to manoeuvre a large box through the now open door. He was carrying a television camera.

"Here, I'll give you a hand with that," said Chas picking up the equipment box and moving through the door onto the platform, saying over his shoulder, "You'll miss the big moment if you don't hurry."

As Chas emerged, the platform erupted in a big cheer. He looked down the length of the train trying to catch a glimpse of whoever the big star was that everyone was waiting for. Anne stepped off behind the camera man who struggled with his rig.

Chas looked at all the people to see what they were focussed on but they were all seemed to be looking at him or the cameraman. The band struck up O' Canada.

Everyone seemed to have a Canadian flag, and a banner was unfurled from the facing of the station wall, which said "Bienvenue, Charles Stuart, Hero of Ver-Sur-Mer.

"What? There must be some mistake," he said to everyone and no one in particular.

A man appeared at his side.

"Monsieur Stuart, welcome to Ver-Sur-Mer, or welcome back for the first time in 40 years. When Mon. Gaspareau told me you were coming, well, I was overcome with joy. Your efforts to save our town and your extraordinary bravery to alert Mon. McAuley to our need will never be forgotten. This station is named Gare McAuley and the street on which it lies is Rue de Charles Stuart."

And so Mayor Jacques Martin of Ver-Sur-Mer directed Chas and Anne down the platform and through the cheering crowds of people. It appeared as if the whole town had turned out for the event. Every child was in their Sunday best, the boys with ties and the girls with flowers in their hair.

Down Rue de Charles Stuart they marched with a band keeping the beat alternating between Le Marseilles and O' Canada. People hung out their upper windows of the small central section of town, straining over the flower boxes to see the parade. In the midst of it all was a still bewildered Chas who wanted nothing more than a quiet afternoon in a small French town. He had come prepared to mourn his comrades.

At the end of the street was an open square with a dais to which Chas and Anne were led. Beside the square was a neatly kept cemetery with rows of white tombstones and a number of larger stone monuments. A small group of war graves were clearly visible from the platform decorated with national flags.

Several dignitaries were seated on the platform and all, save one older man, rose as Chas and Anne ascended the steps.

"Bonjour Madames et Monsieurs," Mayor Martin boomed before switching to English. "I have often longed for this day – to finally have the chance to thank our liberators for their bravery – face to face."

"On that fateful day I was a young boy living on Rue Esmerelda," he waved off to his left and explained for Chas his story as many in town were already familiar with it. "Just over there about a block from the bridge over La Provence. The Canadians saved my life, my family, my town and our beloved France."

Mayor Martin paused remembering a few fateful moments that made up most of his wartime remembrance. A tear gathered in the corner of his eye.

He remembered the day . . . .

**"A Picture of Distance" is the story of three generations of the fictional Stuart family of Toronto. Beginning with their matriarch and ending with her death at nearly 100 years of age, it is the story of the 20th century seen from Canadian eyes.**

**Excerpt from**

# "All Fall Down"

## © F. Bradley Reaume

Three crew members exited the bridge and made their way quickly into the hold. Under a large hatch they made their mechanism ready. One of the crew went immediately to a large cylinder perched on a cradle. He fiddled with controls embedded in it and then patted it, before moving away.

The Sea Merchant continued on the path set by the now dead pilot moving through the Upper Harbour between the Statue of Liberty and Governor's Island towards the middle of the Hudson River. It cleared the southern tip of Manhattan.

The captain had increased the ship's speed to maximum and the ship churned against the current, making its way remorselessly up river. Minutes passed.

The radio crackled to life.

"Sea Merchant, you should be reversing engines to initiate your move to stern. Report."

The captain let the message repeat twice before picking up the radio.

"P-72, we have radio problems. Your signal is not clear. Is it time for reverse engines? Please confirm."

The captain reached for the controls and pressed a button which set the hold cover in motion, once engaged it would open up the cargo bay exposing machinery stored under the deck. The whine of the motors hauling the heavy metal cover away from the large opening in the deck could be heard throughout the ship. Several more minutes passed.

The Sea Merchant had cleared the tip of Manhattan and was passing the North Cove Yacht Harbour.

An explosion on the bow stunned the ship. Small explosions and shrapnel ripped through the bridge followed by a  roar of jet engines. Two F18s flared out over head, now visible through the shattered glass of the bridge as they made their way up the Hudson. They made to turn for a second pass.

The captain grabbed the internal radio control. "Fire!"

The F18 pilots had located the ship, their first rocket had hit the bow in an attempt to disable the screw.  As they passed they saw the opening in the deck. The fighters fired their first close range volley into the control tower to attempt to kill anyone there and further disable the ship. Two Port Authority speed boats were making their way to the Sea Merchant as the jets passed overhead.

Since Rome and the near miss in London the previous year, western port operations were sensitive to anomalies in procedure. The F18s could be on scene within minutes of getting the call. Other defensive measures were also engaged.

The jets wheeled around to challenge the tanker ship again. Both pilots expected to again pepper the control tower, and then swing around to fire rockets at the screw, just under the waterline in the stern. However, both  pilots had seen the open hold and the strange contraption inside.

"Shit, Red Leader what was that?" the question was unnecessary as both pilots knew what they faced.

They had to target ship's command and the hold on their second pass. They made calibration adjustments as they turned to bear down on the Sea Merchant.

The planes took deadly seconds to turn around. As the fighters approached the ship, the large metal cylinder in the hold was flung skyward by the contraption it was resting in. The first F18 pilot couldn't target it as he was locked in on the ship and was too close to recalibrate his target. He fired anyway, as he had no other shot. Two rockets exploded against the bridge and two more entered the hold area.

The rockets hit amidships, into the open hatch and exploded convulsing the deck. A small dingy was nestled under the ship's port side and a few men had jumped aboard. Red Leader had seen the men flee the tanker and wondered for a moment what they were doing.

A Port Authority speedboat approached the Sea Merchant and shots pinged off their boat. They returned fire to the deck edge of the ship and swung around the larger cargo ship to see men boarding the dingy. They squeezed off a few rounds before more shots came their way, causing them to duck and take cover as they rounded the bow.

The second fighter pilot was also targeted on the ship but with more time to react as the cylinder rose he flipped quickly to manual and let off a stream of rounds aimed at the cylinder as it climbed into the air. His desperation, coupled with the speed of his jet and proximity to the new target guaranteed his miss.

The metal cylinder, about seven meters in length, and not quite two meters in diameter, glinted in the sun as it slowed, reaching the height of its upward thrust. It looked like someone had flung a piece of sewer pipe into the air.

Some New Yorkers with a view of the river watched the dance between the jets, the ship and its cargo with only the faintest idea of the drama was occurring. A few knew what they watched and simply held firm, unable to take their eyes off the drama. Most New Yorkers only heard the sounds, which reminded them of the September 11th airplane attack.

The cylinder hung over the river, pausing briefly as it lost the last of its upward momentum and began to fall back to earth. The second F18 pilot exhaled as he banked his plane over the Statue of Liberty and turned towards the Jersey Shore, now two miles away from the river, then three, then four.

The Red Leader F18 pilot had banked the other way over Brooklyn and had turned back toward Manhattan when a sunburst filled his screen. He was flying at nearly the speed of sound directly into a nuclear fireball. He pulled on his controls in a hopeful but ultimately inconsequential attempt to survive.

The second pilot was moving away from the explosion when he saw the flash of light coming from behind. He continued to fly away from the scene waiting for the inevitable shock wave.

As the cylinder rose against the backdrop of Manhattan, the crew screamed "Allahu Akbar". The captain clicked off a text message . . . "It is done." As he pressed 'send', the bomb exploded.

The presence of fighter jets had alerted many New Yorkers to the drama in the Hudson. Many thousands could see the ship and witnessed the attacks from the fighters. Many saw the cylinder rise from the ship and could feel their chests tighten - not really knowing why, but fearing the worst.

The cylinder had reached just over 400 feet in altitude, falling back about 35 feet before exploding. Watching from the upper floors of many Manhattan skyscrapers the skirmish on the Hudson was small and far away given the vast scope of the city spread out beneath them. The cylinder reached up only as high as some of the smaller skyscrapers in its vicinity.

Millions were vaporized as the air itself burned. With temperatures rivaling the center of the sun, metal and glass melted, the water in concrete and mortar boiled and exploded. The air itself was consumed with the resulting shock wave, first pushing everything outward and then rapidly pulling it back in as the air itself rushed in to replace that which was consumed.

The southern half of Manhattan was utterly destroyed. The huge build-ings were shattered and tumbled like children's building bricks and what wasn't vaporised was pushed into the East River. Buildings provided a backdrop against which the shock wave pushed and the rubble piled up against rubble. The southern tip of Manhattan was stripped clean. The built up section of the Jersey shore suffered the same fate.

In Mid-Town, Brooklyn and the further Jersey Shore the stripped land gradually gave way to rubble and remains, with construction materials pummelled, crushed and pushed out from the center of the blast. Temperatures set everything on fire with much of the fire damage confined to the fringes of the damage zone leaving Queen's, Brooklyn and large parts of Bayonne, Jersey City and Union City a raging inferno quickly devoid of most of the millions who had lived there.

"New York control to Delta 455 we are handing you over to the JFK Tower - on Radio five - zero -niner. Safe trav . . . "

"Oh my," said the Delta captain as he saw the flash wash across his windshield from the south of his plane's approach. He signalled his co-pilot, "Raise New York control." He began a turn to the south.

"New York this is Delta 455 we just saw a huge flash . . . oh my God," he trailed off, the beginnings of a mushroom cloud were rising in the distance.

"Try them again, and if there is no response try JFK."


**"All Fall Down" is a story of a nuclear terrorist attack on the United States and the aftermath as issues of revenge, justice, economics, and politics all converge to create a new future.**

An excerpt from

# 'Casting Giant Shadows'

## © F. Bradley Reaume

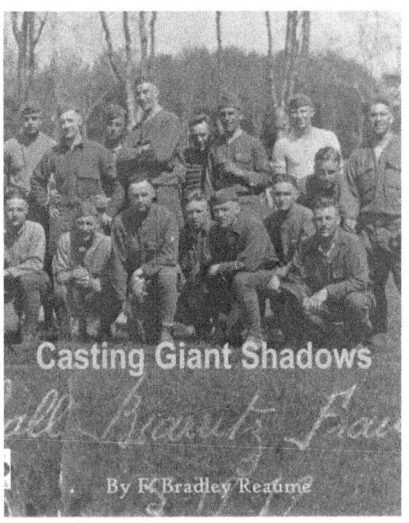

The troop ship sailed triumphantly into New York harbour, sounding its horns, with the deck full of happy soon-to-be ex-soldiers. Fire boats launched a celebratory spray into the air. An unflappable Lady Liberty watched the joyful proceedings.

The ship docked and disgorged its    passengers to a general liberty. A formal leave taking would begin the next day and the ship would remain in New York as a floating hotel for three days while all the men made arrangements to travel from New York to their home towns across the country. Eisenrick invited the platoon to his family bakery early the next day before they all began to get shipped out the following morning.

"I won't pass that up, Frankie," said Jocko Rollins. "I'm guessing your mom makes better stuff than you. I'd like a little bit of heaven before I head home to Missouri."

Momma Eisenrick faced quite a sight at precisely 0-800. She had just completed the rush of morning orders and was standing behind the counter with her head down, thinking of her next task, when a noise caused her to look up from her ledgers as she was reorganizing her mind for the morning.

The boys worked it perfectly. The entire platoon entered the bakery by the front customer entrance, filling the small sit down area where croissants, bread and pastries were sold to walk-in customers each morning. There was a huge hubbub of noise and confusion as they all piled in, much to Mrs. Eisenrick's amusement and consternation. She knew a troop ship had landed the previous evening, in fact it was a regular occurrence.

She put her index fingers to the sides of her mouth and whistled loudly, instantly quieting the hubbub. "What can I get you boys this morning?"

Clancy chimed up, speaking his lines, "We're looking for Frankie. He promised us a bun, like he used to make us in France."

"Oh, you know him? I'm afraid my Frankie hasn't arrived home yet," she said with a sad shake of her head.

Then the door to the ovens behind the counter burst open.

"Momma, momma, I see you've met my friends," said Frankie, who had quickly snuck in the back way through the delivery doors and donned an apron. "I promised them an Eisenrick apple pastry for bringing me home safely." He smiled a huge smile.

His mother began to shake. Her eyes welled up with tears which rolled down her face as her feet were rooted to the floor. The room was silent. Her legs felt like over-cooked spaghetti.

"Oh Frankie, you're home, you're safe and you're whole. And you promised pastries to these boys for brining you home. That's all?" She threw her arms around him and hugged him tight, but only for a moment to make sure he was real. She caught herself, wiped the tears from her eyes and cheeks and mastered herself to take a stern look at her son.

"That's all?" She grabbed trays of pastries and put them up on the counter. "Please, eat. Everyone of you, eat with my thanks for bringing my boy home safely."

A huge cheer went up and Mrs. Eisenrick hugged Frankie again, all the harder.

"Fire up the ovens we are going to need another round of morning pastries," she yelled into the back part of the shop, always the pragmatist. The pastries disappeared in moments so more croissants found their way from the ovens and were offered and then bread was cut, slathered thick with butter. The late morning orders would be a bit behind that day.

"What's all the commotion?" asked a greying man, coming through the oven entrance to the sales area. He was wearing a heavy coat, fresh back from deliveries.

He spied Frankie still being clung to by his mother.

"Father, I am home."

The elder Eisenrick took a step back, blinked a few times and then flung his arms around his son's head. "Safe, as I always knew you would be." He recovered himself quickly. "When can you start delivering for me?"

Everyone laughed.

The Eisenrick's afternoon customers received their orders a bit late that day, but not one was upset once they were informed of Frankie's return. He was well known to their customers.

The next day as they left the ship, the Eisenrick's had made sure that every member of Frankie's platoon took with them a fresh loaf of bread and a bag of pastries for their journey.

One by one the platoon members took their leave, most bidding farewell and reminding each other of their promise to their Captain to meet again in 10 years.


**"Casting Giant Shadows" is the story of an American platoon serving in France in World War One and their friendships and lives after the war.**

**An excerpt from**

## "Past Immortal As We"

© **F. Bradley Reaume**

"Okay, sorry about that, I have too much to think on. I have an exam in particle physics tomorrow and I brought my notes to review while I'm here."

"Ethan?"

"These exams are murder. First thing in the morning, I'm a mess, can't think straight until at least noon. At least it all makes sense, even if the details sometimes elude . . ."

"Ethan?"

"Yes John, what is it?"

"Take a look for yourself," John Overholt was standing in front of the desk and gestured down to the terminal in front of him. John's height lent him an air of being a bit laconic most times. He would never have interrupted even a waitress reciting the daily specials, and his interruption caught Ethan.

With a quizzical look on his face, which consisted mostly of a wry smile and severely crinkled eyes, Ethan moved to the desk. He was shorter than John, though pretty much everyone was shorter than John. He had dark hair which he wore a bit longer than most and combed back with only the slightest touch of gel. Jeans and a button up, collared shirt completed the graduate student ensemble.

"Don't tell me a gremlin got into the data sets. Have you gone and physically looked at the dish to see if it is working alright?"

"A gremlin, that's it. A gremlin that can multiply prime numbers."

Ethan's gaze narrowed. He moved his shorter body to the chair and slid in. He focused on the screen. He was silent for a long while.

His voice was quiet, "I take it you've checked for anomalies? Checked for computer function, the electronics and checked the array? Overholt nodded.

Ethan hadn't taken his eyes from the screen.

"That pretty much settles it. First Contact. Now they'll pull our SETI money."

Overholt couldn't help but laugh. "I doubt that. But I do like the fact that you have made First Contact, the most momentous moment in human history, all about you."

Harendez smiled. "No matter what happens, it's always all about me. The world laps its waves on my shore; I got that from a poem somewhere."

"It's nice to know that the liberal arts have had their impact on even the most cynical science student."

"Let's not take too much of a leap. I think I read it in middle school."

"Apparently your most productive education. And what else have you retained from those halcyon days?"

"I can multiply. So, thinking on it again, now I think they'll double our SETI money. First Contact leads to two way communications and then eventually a face to face visit. Right?"

"First Contact Ethan. Let's just take our time on this one. Unless I miss my guess, these signals seem to be coming from an Earth-like planet about 5.5 light years away. Close cosmologically but still a bit far for us to travel to easily."

"Who are they? What do they want? What does this number sequence mean?"

"I'm glad you asked," said Overholt. "So I will tell you. I have had several hours to puzzle it out."

Ethan's eyes went wide. Overholt stared at Ethan, preparing to speak, but didn't. Ethan looked at Overholt's forced bovine calm and they both began to laugh. They laughed loud long and nervously, realizing as they did, that they were at the center of a maelstrom of publicity and science which would wash over them, consume them and spit them out very much changed, as the astonishing news spread.

For now, they alone knew the future. It wouldn't stay that way for long. Knowing the report would generate a call from the Head of the Department, a nano-second after he read it, John waited at the array, enjoying the effect his news would have on his supervisor, the President of the University and everyone as it rippled out across the whole world. He texted Allie, wanting her to know but swearing her to secrecy.

And Ethan couldn't stop talking about the inevitable media interviews, and practicing his responses. And they laughed and laughed, giddy at the sudden ridiculousness of it all.

**"Past Immortal As We" is a science fiction story about First Contact with an alien intelligence and how humanity copes with the rapid changes in its foundations.**

**Excerpted from**

# 'Becoming'

© F. Bradley Reaume

"We are staying on I-95 South so just follow the signs. We might be catching the back bit of the morning rush."

The highway snaked through some neighbourhoods, with highways, arterial roads and local exits every half a mile or so. Andrew watched, intently scanning the traffic and the overhead signs, smoothly swinging through the traffic. As the river harbor became more evident to their left, the traffic noticeably thinned giving them a whoosh of freedom as they crossed a bridge which gave them an unobstructed view of the harbour and downtown Jacksonville.

At that moment, three fuel tanker trucks were moving south of the harbour on the east side of the river.

"Holy shit," yelled Andrew a huge plume of fire exploded around either side of the elevated roadway. He mashed the brakes and wrenched the wheel to the right steering into the shoulder to avoid the pick-up truck in front of him.

The car behind him skidded and with nowhere to go, almost stopped before sliding with a crunch of metal into the pick up that Andrew had avoided. Cars and trucks in the left hand lane followed a similar trajectory, with some vehicles angling into the left shoulder, some being pushed into the guard rail and others pan-caking into each other to avoid the carnage.

A couple of fearless, stupid or slow to react drivers slipped through the fireball, either as they had no choice or because they had a clear path with fire towering over either side of the road.

The third tanker truck had driven at speed into the other two, stopped at a light under the highway bridge waiting for the green to continue southbound on the local streets.

Andrew and Diane said nothing as they both assessed the very slowly unfolding scene. A few hardy or crazy souls saw an opening, dislodged themselves from the mass of stopped vehicles and shot forward through the flames and smoke to the safety of the now empty highway in front of them. On the right shoulder, Andrew and Diane were blocked from moving forward by other cars that had become entangled or damaged in the rush to stop.

"You okay Diane?"

"Um, um, yeah. I'm okay. You?"

"Fine. Thankfully we avoided any collision. We can't go until those cars in front of us move. We weren't hit. I'm going to check."

Andrew flicked the latch and quickly got out of the car. He could feel the heat of the fire. A few of the other vehicles were spitting out people, most of whom looked awe struck at the flame perhaps 50 yards in front of them. Some scanned for damage to their own vehicles. The guy in the pick-up was near the back of his truck and looking at the woman in the car which had hit him. The damage to his truck was minor but her car's hood was folded and the front lights and grill were in pieces strewn across the pavement. She waved she was okay but was struggling with the door which was jammed.

The flames and smoke roared and rose with the sound of sirens somewhere off in the distance. Andrew could see the accident scene on the highway was only a few cars deep, as the thinning traffic had allowed those back of the accident to stop before crashing. As traffic had been thin on the south side of downtown, there were no serious collisions, just some twisted metal and jumbled vehicles. There was no way to back out either. Despite avoiding the accident, he was trapped by it.

With nowhere to go Andrew then looked forward past the pick-up to see if it could move. Two vehicles ahead, cars were twisted sideways and the paint on their hoods was blistering off due to the heat. Andrew could feel it, like the sun beating down on you when you already have a sunburn.

However, 50 yards back from the source it didn't seem dangerous. It was almost soothing in the early morning Florida sun.

Then he heard a crackling. Diane had gotten out of the car and was motioning the driver beside them to exit her car from the passenger side.

"I think we need to get out of here," said the driver of the pick-up. "I don't like that sound."

"What about the people in the front cars?"

"You saw the damage. Did you see anyone moving?"

"Diane, get back and move off the road, get down the embankment. I don't know but with the heat and the damage I don't trust our gas tanks. I gotta at least take a look at that front car."

"Andrew be careful." She was shaking as if she'd stepped into a deep freeze. Smoke billowed up from either side of the southbound road.

"Just a quick look."

Carlton ran off, using the cars as a shield. The heat had dissipated as the size of the flame was reduced and was bearable and the smoke drifted lazily off to the north east, but the fire still crackled out of sight beneath the highway, with a lick of flame occasionally becoming visible to those on the highway. Andrew did not know that while one of the tankers had exploded, two others were engulfed in the flame, full of gasoline and leaking badly.

He passed a car where two people had gotten out and he motioned them back. "Get back quick. If there's another explosion it'll burn here."

With a few athletic steps he was at the front car. Through the window he could see three people all unconscious and sweating. He banged on the window. Two adults in the front did not move, but a young girl in the back seat shook her eyes open. She pulled on the door latch and the door opened a bit but was stuck.

Carlton used his left hand to touch the outside latch, for a tiny moment. Even though it faced away from the flame the door was superheated as he expected. He yelled and motioned for the girl to use her feet to kick at the door. She was too spent to be able to put much effort in.

211

He heard a series of pops from under the bridge. He sensed he had to get away quickly.

He took off his shirt and used it as an oven mitt. He grabbed the latch with his left hand and reached into the slight gap where the door had almost opened and pulled quickly and as hard as he could. It moved but did not give way. The shirt smoldered and his fingers burned. He tried again with a last bit of effort as the billowing smoke had increased. Looking around he noticed emergency workers had moved far back of the underpass and were watching it from cover. He knew the fire below was not spent.

He yelled 1-2-3 and together he pulled, the girl pushed and the door popped open. He grabbed her by the wrist, pulled her from the car, threw her over his shoulder and ran back, scrambling down the embankment, gently placing her beside Diane.

"I think I should go back to get the others."

As he started to rise a tremendous explosion ripped the air, blowing flame and heat up and out from the lower roadway as first one tanker exploded and  moments later the second followed. The roadbed convulsed and gave way.

There was a wave of heat and those down the hill cowered into the ground until the blast furnace let up with most of its fuel consumed.

Andrew looked at Diane who appeared to be alright, comforting a small boy with his mother. Andrew noticed that a bit of Diane's shirt had melted into her shoulder. He looked at it long enough to see it was only an inch long section right at the point of her shoulder. She had some light burns on her right arm and neck, but it looked like a moderately bad sunburn.

He reached to touch her and she winced.

"Don't. I'm okay but that blast gave me a singe. It felt like taking too long to light a gas grill. You know, the gas flash as the flame catches the excess gas? I think it burnt off some hair."

Sure enough there were little burnt hairs on her upper arm and evidence of some burnt hair around her ear. There was an ongoing series of pops as the flame licked the underside of the remaining concrete   highway bridge. Water in the concrete was exploding into steam, and failed concrete was falling in bits and chunks from  what remained of the road bed into the conflagration below.

"We need to move further away. We don't know what else is under there."


**'Becoming' is the story of  youths making the difficult choices necessary to face their futures. It focuses on players, coaches and the families attached to a minor professional baseball team as they face the end of the season and look forward to what comes next.**

**Excerpted from**

# 'Reckoner'

### © by F. Bradley Reaume

"Make no mistake Mr. Trewilliger. Everything has been done before. This time, let us do it with a clear head and an approach that acknowledges the interests of all the denizens of Trapten.

"Swizenstien will leave tomorrow morning asking you hold his position here for the next couple of days. You need not have divided loyalties in that time. Once the funerals and mourning periods have ended things in the Manor will find their new normal. A perfect time for you to take on your new role.

At the end of the mourning period, go to your lodgings, retrieve your things and, should you choose, return to your new duties. Your current employer will not be shocked, the same thing was proposed to him 40 years ago. He decided to do his duty to the Estate by remaining with the law firm. He was tied more tightly to the firm as his father was still very much alive. I expect Swizenstien will be happy to believe he has a man inside."

Never being good with revelations I simply clammed up, the feeling on my skin matching that in my head. While it appeared to be done, I strongly believed I had several days in which to change terms, demand clarity, or walk away altogether. And if Agatha was to be believed I had a lifetime to decide as I could always leave. I wasn't sure as the Estate seemed to get into one's blood.

Seeing my future with the law firm rolling out in front of me and contrasting that to the uncertainty of Trapten and the strange behaviour of the place, I had already made my decision but gloried in the pivot point of having choice.

I looked down the verdant bank to the stream. It mumbled along not knowing that it would reach its twin. Looking more closely, I could see the erosion of the bank, a hint of brown grass at the river's edge and a couple of weeds poking out from under the bank. What had seemed so manicured moments before had revealed itself as natural and imperfect.

Agatha asked me to meet with Agnes, as she would want to speak of this new arrangement. I went to her rooms several hours later at the appointed time.

Agnes in her wheelchair beckoned me closer and indicated a chair where I should sit.

The room was dark save for two candles flickering their light at either end of the small room. I tensed as I felt an animal brush up against my leg.

"My father the Earl has upset the order of things." She was distracted and speaking as if someone else's thoughts and her own mind were elsewhere.

Her words barely registered in my brain, still engaged in compartmentalizing my new surroundings.

"But my grandfather has begun to set things straight."

"These people are dead."

"Mr. Trewilliger, you know from firsthand experience that the dead are always with us."

"So," I started, "if the dead are still with us, and you have direct knowledge of the Old Earl, and his father, how is it that you have not the same knowledge of Terrence, Edward and Michael?"

Agnes gave me her full attention and a sour look," Because they have not revealed themselves to me, or presumably to you, or anyone else."

"But they could?"

"Who knows? I am not an expert on the workings of the spirit world. I have only spoken to the dead, I have not understood their social norms or rules under which they are compelled to exist."

"Maybe it's worth asking?"

"I have. And what I do know is that these spirits are not in heaven as we might imagine it. After all, what is heaven, Mr. Trewilliger?

"Do you think it a place where you do what you like all the time? A place where there is competition and passion but without bitterness, loss, fear and remorse?"

"That would be the classic definition, I suppose."

"What I know is that the spirits of the dead linger on to guard or direct the lives of those they cared about in their own lives. They try to help but are not always successful, which is why not all people gain from their existence. Once everyone they knew in life has passed, they no longer have any influence and they are called to the next phase, but no one has returned from that sphere to tell us what to expect."

Agnes merely looked at me as a parent would look at a small child after making a particularly complicated answer as best they can. There was definitely more to it but she was unable or unwilling to try to make me understand.

I was at a loss, and not knowing my next logical step, I remained silent, searching for the proper prod to elicit more detail. And then there was a moaning, well, not really moaning, more like a softly exhaled breath announcing an unknown presence.

"These ghosts do not have the slightest idea of how to manage the Estate," it was the late Earl's voice. "They simply refuse to do what I require of them."

Agnes remained still. The candle behind her also held its form as if air currents in the room had ceased and the flame had no outside force pushing it to flicker.

"The newly arrived do not know about this sphere," said another voice. "I will be moving on now that you have come to take my place. But first I must inform you of your duties."

"But father, I have no duties, save those I choose, not since I was quite young."

"Your duties have always been set by me, even if you did not see them as such in your youth. You are to manage this limited sphere, in this place. You are not the Absolute, which only arrives in time of great need. In time you may become the driver of events, the manager of life and death here at Trapten. You may be bypassed, as I have now been."

While her body sat in the chair I was not sure where Agnes was. Her eyes were closed and she made no motion at the spirit's words. My eyes were wide open and my ears tingling.

A shimmering spot of light moved toward the candle behind Agnes, and then another, and another from a different direction, until the shimmers became a rush from several angles, and the rush condensed into several continuous beams of light shining on the flame.

Once solid, the beams of light seemed to radiate in and out, back and forth for a time and then faded. The candle on the other side of the room flickered continuously, caught in some movement of air that was not apparent to me. I heard nothing more, though Agnes remained seated with her eyes clenched tight, nodding slightly here and there.

It did not seem long until dawn broke the spell.

Agnes opened her eyes, looked around the room until her gaze focussed on me.

"The Old Earl's father, the 21st Earl has imparted his wisdom to his son, my father, the 22nd Earl. The spirits have lined up behind him, out of loyalty at the behest of his father. The spirits are content for now. Only time, circumstance and choice will decide if the late Earl or the new Earl will have a usurper. My grandfather will move on."

I closed my eyes to center my thoughts. When I opened them the room was bright with natural light, the mist on the lawns looked as thin as I'd ever seen it. Agnes was gone.

**"Reckoner" is a neo-gothic story about the nature of good and evil, centered on the doings of an ancient titled family during a transition from one Earl to the next. It's main character is caught in the middle of competing desires and must come to terms with the intervention of the dead, the desires of the living family members and his own future.**

# F. Bradley Reaume

Brad has written his entire career, first as a newspaper reporter and columnist, and then in the political and government world before pursuing fiction.

'The Queen's Keys' is his eighth novel.

Brad lives with his wife and children in Ontario, Canada.

**Also by F. Bradley Reaume**

## Novels

**A Picture of Distance** (2014) - a family saga

**All Fall Down** (2016) - future history after a nuclear attack on New York

**Casting Giant Shadows** (2017) - story of Americans in The Great War

**Past Immortal As We** (2018) - story about alien first contact

**Becoming** (2019) - baseball team players and coaches face their future

**Reckoner** (2020) - odd occurrences at a huge gothic manor house

**The Cup** (2021) - the American frontier shapes those who tame it

## Other Books

**A Wander Within Wonder (2021) -** verse and prose telling of an epic tale

**Other Skylines** (2015) - short stories

**The Wonderful World of Wogs** (2014) - illustrated for pre-schoolers

*** As Brad Reaume / Illustrated by Nicole Flax